*For my sister, Shirley, and those Saturday morning films with
Roy Rogers, White Eagle and The Durango Kid which first
aroused my interest in the American West.*

PROLOGUE

A wind blew along Missoula's main street, coming from the north, bringing with it an icy foretaste of the winter to come. The rattle of loose planks and ill-fitting window frames added a tympanic rhythm to the occasional bugle bellow as it blew through the mountain pass above the town. Black clouds hung low overhead, moving fast like thirsty cattle with the scent of a river in their nostrils, rushing to the promise of something better ahead, and though it was barely two hours past midday they darkened the town, draining every colour to grey. Most residents remained within their own homes. A few cattlemen, wary of the power of the elements and reluctant to subject themselves or their horses to the trial of returning to their ranch, played cards in one saloon or another. Experience told them that such a wind would blow itself out in a couple of hours. The tradespeople stuck to their task although the storekeeper, barber, haberdasher and others had no hope of any more business this day.

The door of the sheriff's office, too, was closed tightly

and the two men within sat cosily near the stove drinking coffee and eating biscuits that Deputy Fred Skinner's new wife had insisted he bring with him that morning. The cells were empty and had been for several days. 'One thing about the winter,' Sheriff Martin remarked, 'people seem more reluctant to break the law. Less drunkenness. Fewer fights.'

'Because the cowboys don't come to town as much,' Fred replied. 'Guess they have as many fights but when they happen on the ranch we don't get to hear about them.'

Billy Martin nodded his head slowly; a sage like acceptance of his deputy's words. 'You got something there, Fred.' He paused. 'Still,' he added, 'times are changing. Five years ago Missoula was a bad town summer and winter. The place was full of gunmen. Shoot-outs were a regular event.'

'Why was that?' Fred didn't really need to ask the question; Billy Martin had supplied the answer every time he'd told one of his stories. But Fred liked to listen to the sheriff's tales and Billy certainly enjoyed telling them. Fred's words had been nothing more than a prompt to get his boss to fill in the afternoon with a few more reminiscences.

Billy Martin smiled. 'Up here among the hills was a good place to lie low. Men stopped here as they headed west to escape crimes they'd committed in the eastern states, and outlaws from Oregon and Idaho made for here on their way east. Some travelled north, into Canada. As long as they weren't wanted for a crime in Montana they could stay here as long as they cared to.'

He poured more coffee into his tin mug. ''Course there was often trouble when gunmen arrived in town at the same time. The winner was usually invited to leave before sundown.' He sniffed. 'Quite a few tough men buried up on the hill yonder.'

Fred wandered over to the window and duly inspected what was happening out on the street. A couple of men had arrived in town and were attempting to tie their horses to the hitching rail outside the bank, which was on the opposite side of the street and a couple of blocks down. A sudden blast of wind tugged at the skirt of their long coats, and each clamped a hand to his head to prevent the loss of his hat. Their horses shied and pulled making it difficult for the dismounted riders to hitch them. Finally they succeeded and stepped up onto the boardwalk. Fred watched as the two men parted; one heading further down the main street like he was seeking out a saloon, while the other took the narrow street along the side of the bank and was soon out of sight.

'What's happening?' asked Billy Martin.

'Strangers,' Fred answered and described what the two men were doing. Billy grunted and offered a coffee refill to his deputy, who went back to the stove with his empty cup.

While the two lawmen kept warm within the main street office, two more riders arrived in Missoula. They, too, dismounted outside the bank and tied their horses to the same hitching rail the first strangers had used. All four men were tall but one, the eldest, was stout while the others were slim. The eldest man paused on the board-walk and stretched his back as he looked up and down the street. Momentarily he caught the attention of the first two arrivals then, followed by the fourth man, he went into the bank.

Thadeus Clayton had had a chip on his shoulder for twenty years, ever since he'd lost his land to Union carpetbaggers at the end of the Civil War. In the intervening years he'd stolen money from every likely source; stagecoaches, trains and banks. He'd had a simple philosophy; commit the crimes in one state then cross the line to another where the law couldn't follow. When his notoriety made raiding in one state too dangerous, he moved on, further west or north. Now he was picking on the money carriers in Montana.

In the early years he'd worked alone but with his wife now dead and his sons old enough to ride a horse and carry a gun, crime was a family business. Their involvement, however, was more a case of necessity than a means of extending his range of activities. None of his sons had an ounce of intelligence and were capable of nothing but the simplest task. Ezra, who now accompanied him into the bank, was the smartest of the three, but even he hadn't the ability to plan a raid nor the sense to avoid a posse on their trail. Without their pa the boys would be swinging on a gallows tree within a week. Even with him, he sometimes thought that their presence on a raid was tantamount to putting a noose around everyone's neck. Outside he'd found it necessary to pause on the boardwalk to catch Algy's attention. Instead of being ready to act as a lookout during the robbery his youngest boy had allowed himself to be distracted by something he'd seen in a store window. They'd arrived in town in separate

10

pairs to give the impression they didn't know each other but Thad's need to prompt Algy could have destroyed all that. He could only hope that the sheriff, like the rest of the citizens of Missoula, was too preoccupied with keeping warm to notice the behaviour of newcomers.

Thad Clayton's plan was simple enough. When the bank was empty he and Ezra would force the teller to pack their saddle-bags. If any of the townsfolk entered the bank while the robbery was in progress then either Algy or Barney would follow them in and prevent them from raising an alarm. If they could get clear of the town without any commotion then Thad was sure they would evade capture. He had a hideout already prepared where they could wait until the immediate hue and cry was over.

It seemed to be their lucky day. The bank was empty and, because of the bitter chill of the day, the woollen scarves which were wrapped around the lower part of their faces didn't seem out of place.

'How can I help you, gentlemen?' asked the teller.

Behind the teller the door to a vault stood open and a second man could be seen crouched on the floor struggling with a large, metal strongbox.

Thad threw the saddle-bags he had brought with him onto the counter and drew his gun. 'You can fill these with all the money you've got.'

Ezra dropped his saddle-bags beside his father's then pressed the barrel of his gun to the top of the teller's nose, between his eyes. 'Quick as you can,' he said.

The two bank employees needed no other instruction. If either of them had any thought of resisting the robbers it stayed in their head. Thad had never known a robbery

11

go with such ease before. 'Don't come outside 'til we're clear of the street,' Thad warned as he backed towards the door. 'I've got men watching this door. They'll shoot if you come out too soon.' The last sentence was merely for effect; all four Claytons would ride out of Missoula together, but if the bank employees believed they would be killed by opening the door too quickly it would give Thad and his boys a start that would be good enough to thwart the effort of any posse assembled to catch them. Pushed as far as Montana there were now few states that they were able to enter with impunity and further bloodshed would only increase the law's desire to hunt them down.

With filled saddle-bags in hand, father and son left the bank and made for the horses. Barney, Ezra's twin, was in place, lounging against a post which supported a first floor balcony. His nervous look told Thad that all was not well. He looked to the corner where Algy should have been on guard but his youngest son wasn't there. In answer to his pa's angry question Barney gave an awkward shrug; he didn't know what had happened to his brother.

Liquorice sticks and humbugs were the cause of Algy's desertion. He'd always had a sweet tooth and the display of jars and boxes in the general store window had, at that moment, offered a promise of delight which was in excess of anything he'd ever seen before. He'd become engrossed by them, selecting those he'd come back and buy after he'd got his share of the money from the robbery. His pa always gave him some dollars to spend after they'd done a job. Thinking of his pa, Algy turned his head from the window and looked back to the junction with the main street. He was surprised to see his pa there and, judging by his splayed leg stance and lowered eyebrows, he was not pleased with his son. Algy hadn't meant to stay away from the front of the bank when his pa and Ezra arrived. He figured they'd got into town sooner than they'd said they would. He nodded to his pa to let him know he was on his way to take up his position. Just one more look in the window to remind himself of those striped humbugs, they were his favourite sweet. But then he saw the jar up high filled with different coloured beans. How had he missed those? The red ones looked full of flavour. He couldn't stop himself licking his lips. There was a whole lot more up on that shelf. He counted the jars and studied the contents working out which were chewy, which were crunchy and which had hard-toffee centres. There were boxes, too; fancy boxes with ribbons and bows which held pink and white candies. He smiled at the thought of spending half-an-hour alone in there, but right at this moment he didn't have half an hour to spare. Once more his glance shifted to the junction with the main street and he could see the horses moving. His pa and brothers were mounted, preparing to ride away. He shook his head in disbelief. They hadn't had time to rob the bank, had they?

Knowing he would have incurred the anger of his father and brothers for not being where he should have been when they left the bank, Algy began to run along the narrow street. Suddenly, the side door of the bank building opened. One of the tellers stepped outside, his back to Algy. In his hands he held a double-barrelled shotgun. Instantly he fired one barrel into the air and yelled, 'Robbery,' as soon as the resulting air reverberations had stilled enough for his voice to be heard. He fired the second barrel, determined that the citizens of the town would know what was happening at their bank.

The mounted Claytons appeared at the mouth of the side street. They could see the teller with his now useless weapon and beyond him they could see the fourth member of their family. 'Come on, Algy,' yelled his father who was still hopeful of getting clear of Missoula before a gunfight ensued.

But Algy changed all that. The fact that the teller had discharged both barrels had no significance for him. All he knew was that someone from the bank was firing a gun and he assumed the target was either his pa or his brothers. 'Hey,' he shouted, while pulling his own pistol from its holster. Algy wasn't a quick draw but in this instance he didn't need to be. He was, however, accurate and his first shot struck the teller in the chest, spinning him dramatically before he fell. He was dead, or dying, before he hit the ground but Algy plugged him again as he ran past, the bullet striking the stricken man in the centre of his forehead.

By now men curious to know the cause of the shotgun fire were appearing on Missoula's main street. The teller's cry of, 'Robbery!' had been heard and was running along the street like a prairie fire. Thad Clayton's frantic arm waving to hurry Algy to his horse gave them a location on which to focus their attention.

Someone shouted for them to surrender but Ezra Clayton drew his six-gun and fired in that direction. He

14

missed, clipping a splinter from a porch post outside the Lariat Saloon. Men ran for cover while reaching for their weapons. Lead zipped along the main street as the Claytons spurred their horses south. Algy, having dashed from the narrow side street, his eyes bright with excitement, was shouting, 'Hi-yeee!' like an outrider driving strays back to the herd.

Bullets whistled past the horses and over the heads of the riders as they tried to pick up speed. Ezra turned in his saddle and fired back along the street at one citizen who had evacuated the protection of a water trough in order to give himself a clearer shot at the fleeing robbers. Ezra's bullet tore into his shoulder and left him writhing on the ground.

Fred Skinner and Sheriff Billy Martin had dropped their cups of coffee at the sound of the bank teller's first alarm shot. Fred was on the boardwalk outside their office, gun in hand, watching their approach. He noted the similarity of appearance of the three younger men and guessed at the identity of the bank robbers. A shot took away a lump of material from the brim of his hat. He stood his ground and fired three shots from his revolver. Then Billy Martin's rifle thundered to his left and they saw the eldest member of the gang lurch with the impact of the bullet. He would almost certainly have fallen if one of the others hadn't grabbed his coat and kept him in the saddle. There was no more shooting after that, the four keeping low to reduce the possibility of another hit.

'It was the Clayton gang,' Fred Skinner announced. 'I recognized the twins from the posters we've got.'

'See how many men you can round up for a posse,' Billy Martin ordered his deputy. 'Don't suppose we'll get far before there's no light at all for tracking, but one of them is hit and it could have slowed them down. I reckon they were heading east so you'd better get telegraphs off to the sheriffs at Wicker and Bridger Butte. Warn them to be on the lookout.'

CHAPTER ONE

Jess Clarke worked quickly, hands and eyes checking the harness that coupled the dun pair to the flat wagon. They were restless. Hoofs stamped and scraped. Heads tossed as snorts and snickers declared their unease. Jess spoke quietly, soothing the animals while he examined the straps and buckles. He ran his hands over their flanks and down their legs and, when at last satisfied with their fitness and his own endeavour, he stood before them and rubbed each muzzle in a last gesture of assurance.

From the narrow porch of their bleached, timber home, Mary Clarke watched her son's effort to keep the team in check. The wind blew. The horses shied. Mary lifted her gaze to the mountains, the peaks of which were lost in black cloud. In keeping with the last three days, there was little daylight. Winter was coming early and the threatening storm, which had the animals spooked, was no less alarming to Mary. She remembered the winter five years ago. That, too, had been early and severe. According to the old-timers, that was the pattern of things. An early winter was always a hard winter and it was seldom the herald of an early spring. For weeks, that

17

year, they had been isolated on their farm. Dark days, struggling to eke out provisions for the family and tending to the small number of cattle and horses that were close enough to benefit from the fodder in the barn. The suddenness of that winter had caught out every settler, none of whom had been able to collect their full herd near enough to the ranch house. Frozen carcasses, those of the cattle which hadn't fallen to voracious wolves, were a cruel find when it was once more possible to ride the range. And now, Mary thought, just as the bank loan needed to see them through the following lean years had been repaid, it looked like happening again.

As he approached the house calling for his pa, Mary's attention returned to her son. Despite her current concerns she was proud of Jess. Proud that he had grown tall and strong, proud of his diligence around the farm and proud of the growing respect his neighbours had for him. Jess was eighteen years old but had already adopted his father's love of the land, knowledge of the stock and good-humoured determination to see a job done. Rarely did she visit the township of Wicker without someone speaking in praise of him. But in the past two weeks, since his pa, Matt, had suffered a broken arm, he had taken the weight of responsibility in his stride. No-one lauded his efforts more than his parents.

'Team's hitched,' Jess shouted in the direction of the open farm house door. His father emerged almost instantly with a heavy outdoor coat draped across his shoulders and an expression across his face which bespoke his frustration at his inability to fasten it. Matt

Clarke was a self-sufficient man. He had settled alone on this parcel of land. For the first three years he had cleared it, ploughed it, planted and harvested without help from anyone. Then he'd married Mary and while she raised children he continued to raise crops and cattle. A small herd at first, but large enough to make him proud of his achievement and instil in him the determination to develop his land into a spread that would sustain his children and their children in the years ahead. In his opinion, working from sunup to sundown was an investment greater than money. Not only did it keep him active and in control of the events on his farm, but it also ensured his awareness of changes and threats before they had time to develop into trouble.

Even so, he'd been fortunate. In twenty-three years on this land nothing had knocked him off his feet. Neither accident nor illness had prevented him working his land nor bad weather from tending whatever stock he could reach. A bullet had scorched his ribs in a skirmish with rustlers, a bull steer had pressed him against a corral post and riding accidents had jarred, bruised and gashed his body on several occasions, but nothing kept him abed or idle or unable to handle his own business. Not until he broke his arm. Now he couldn't even fasten his coat without someone's help, and needing assistance didn't sit easy with him. Nor did the fact that his wife and son found some amusement in his incapacity.

'There!' said Mary after she'd got his left arm into its sleeve and had pulled the coat over his right shoulder, fastening the buttons with the sling-tied right arm trapped inside. She put a glove on his left hand and smiled up at him when he grumped at her administration. 'Jess'll look after you,' she said as he headed towards the wagon.

He stopped, turned back, the words almost out of his mouth that he didn't need anyone to look after him when he realized she was teasing him and the stern lines about his face relaxed. 'I won't always be like this,' he said, trying to move his right arm to show her of what he was speaking.'

'I should hope not,' she said gently.

'In fact,' said Matt, 'when we get to town I'll go see the doctor. See if I can get rid of this strapping.'

'It's only been on two weeks. He told you it would be at least four.'

'Yeah. Well, I'll offer him twice his fee. Perhaps then he'll half the time. Doctors,' he muttered, 'only want you to go back so they can charge you another fee.'

'Nonsense, Matt. Doctor Hames is a good man. You do what he tells you otherwise you might end up with a permanently weak arm. Give it the proper time to heal.'

Matt grumped again but Mary wasn't sure if it was in response to her words or due to the effort of hauling himself one-handed onto the driving board. As Jess set himself to climb up beside his father, his mother caught hold of his sleeve. 'Here,' she said, draping a long, woollen scarf around his neck. 'It's a north wind. You'll need all the protection you can get when you reach the valley.' To emphasize the point she pulled the flaps of his fleece-lined, leather cap over his ears.

Jess was as embarrassed as his father by his mother's fussing but he tried not to let it show. He wrapped the scarf once around his neck simply to please her. 'We shouldn't be more than four hours,' he told her as he clambered aboard and gathered up the reins. She nodded and stepped clear of the horses as her son flipped the leathers to urge them forward. From the raised veranda she watched the wagon travel slowly down to the ford then climb again at the far side of the river where the turnoff to their ranch joined the trail to town. As she looked again toward the mountains and the dark, foreboding sky she sensed the presence of her daughter behind her.

'Is there a storm coming, Ma?' Clara put her arm around her mother's waist. She was thirteen, skinny, as Jess had been at that age, but blessed with a smile that could win any argument with her father.

'Reckon so,' said Mary, 'but the men folk will soon be back and we'll all be safe inside until it blows itself out.'

There were barely enough buildings in Wicker for it to deserve the term 'town' although it had grown somewhat from the little group of log cabins of that first established trading post forty years earlier. Mountain men and Indians had met here to barter and the mountain men had taken to calling the place *wiccaothi*, which is the Sioux name for a village or camp, and over the years the name had been distorted and Anglicized so that newcomers from the east mistakenly thought that the settlement had been founded by a man called Wicker. That was how the first sign writer had written the name and now they were stuck with it. It was well sited at the base of the Bitterroot mountains and on the bank of the

Dearborn River barely a dozen miles from its confluence with the Missouri. The old hunters, both red and white, had brought to the trading post a plentiful supply of beaver and otter pelts, bear skins and antelope hides, but, when the war between the States was over, a new fashion in the east reduced the value of beaver skins and the heyday of the mountain man was over. Gone, also, were the assemblies with tribesmen who no longer came to barter. Civilization had brought with it fear and distrust of the red men who now stayed in their villages watching with growing concern as the white men slaughtered the buffalo on the plains, taking only the pelt, leaving the flesh and bones to rot on the open land.

Gone, too, from Wicker, were the log cabins. They had been replaced by fifty or more high, wood frame buildings which spread, haphazardly, along the river bank. Most of them wore a coat of whitewash or pale coloured paint, protection against the extreme elements that were a part of that sparsely populated area of the untamed land west of the Missouri. Some of those buildings were hung with signs – Lucy's Boarding House, Jail, Stable and Blacksmith – but the largest building and the focal point of the town was the emporium run by Lars Freidrikson.

Lars and his family lived in the upstairs rooms. By far, the greatest portion of the ground floor of the emporium was taken up with his stock of essential supplies, goods required by every family in the valley. The store was well organized. There were sections for hardware, clothing, dry goods, canned foods, paint, wire and fancy goods. In addition, Lars kept several copies of the *Sears and Roebuck* catalogue so that his customers could order special items at any time. He kept a desk and a chair in a distant corner to ensure privacy for anyone selecting goods in this manner, however it didn't prevent him wanting to know every detail appertaining to the purchase – which member of the family was to be the recipient of the gift or what occasion had prompted such a purchase.

The remainder of the ground floor was a saloon bar, access to which was either by a connecting door from the storehouse or a street door at the front of the building. It was a long, narrow section of the building with a bare wood counter opposite the door to the storehouse and five tables spaced along the adjoining wall. Lars served the beers at night when the storehouse was closed but employed Brigg Hutton as barman during the day. For many years it had been the only liquor selling establishment in Wicker, the place where the men met to drink and gamble, argue and cuss. Women didn't go in there except for town socials and town meetings. Over the years few of either had been held there; dances were usually held in the summer and outdoors and public meetings were considered unnecessary. The accepted rule was that people made their own law. Disputes were settled between opposing parties without interference from others. The jail was there to hold drunks overnight. Justice, for anything more serious, like rustling, horse stealing and murder, was meted out by the injured party.

It was to the emporium that Jess Clarke directed the horses, pulling them to a halt at the front of the building then guiding them backwards down the side alley, seeking to get the wagon as near as possible to the storehouse door for loading. It wasn't a simple manoeuvre; two wagons were already in position near the boardwalk and being loaded with provisions. 'We're not the only family expecting the storms to keep us tied to the ranch,' said Matt. 'That's Hurd Baker's team,' he indicated a partially loaded wagon, 'and the Flynn family behind.' Jess was well aware which wagon teams belonged to which family and nodded an acknowledgement of his father's words while he hitched their own team to a rail. Matt spoke again. 'Looks like we'll be here longer than we expected. Could be another thirty minutes before Lars gets around to filling our order.' Gingerly, he climbed down from the wagon and turned up the collar of his big coat. He looked up at the sky. 'Beginning to snow,' he said, his voice sounding easy but it didn't hide his concern from Jess.

'Ma and Clara will be OK 'til we get home.'

'Reckon so,' he said, craning his neck to peer through the doorway into the emporium. There was lot of activity, townspeople in there as well as the two farmers whose wagons were to be loaded ahead of their own. 'Might just have a walk down to the doc's place. See if I can get rid of this sling. I'll be a sight more useful without it.'

Jess tried to dissuade him, told him he could manage the heavy stuff until Matt was fit again, but his pa went nonetheless. 'Let Lars know we're here. You know what we need if I'm not back, don't you?'

Jess did and went inside to wait his turn.

Lars and his wife and his eldest son were all tending customers so Jess occupied himself looking at the new Colt revolvers – the .45 calibre Single Action Army

Revolver known as the Peacemaker. Jess and his pa had inspected them the last time they'd been in Wicker. Lars told them they were selling faster than rustled cattle. Although they had only been available for a few months, demand had been so high that Lars had submitted several requisitions to maintain a minimum stock level. Jess could understand why. The gun fascinated him. One of the models was nickel plated and shone like silver, and to add to its allure it was fitted with ivory grips on the butt. But fancy goods didn't impress Jess. For him the one with the blue barrel and walnut handle appeared much more sturdy, more capable of fulfilling its intended function. If he was ever going to carry a sidearm then that was the gun for him.

'Is that the first item on your list?' Lars Friedrikson's light voice, heavy with its Scandinavian lilt, interrupted the lad's inspection.

Jess grinned. He knew the storekeeper well enough to know when he was being teased. 'Perhaps one day, Mr Freidrikson. For now there's a whole lot of provisions needed to see us through the next few weeks. If we get cut off from town a new gun won't feed us no matter how shiny it is or quick to load and fire.' Although he knew what he said was true there was still a wistful element in the last look he gave the weapons before turning his full attention to supplying the list of goods they had come to collect.

'Where's your pa?' Lars asked.

'Went to see the doctor about his arm. Convinced himself that the quicker he pays the bill the quicker his arm will heal.'

Lars laughed. 'An impatient man, your father.' At that moment he spotted Matt Clarke in the entranceway looking for his son. Snow lay on the crown and brim of his hat. The shoulders of his coat were damp where snow had melted. 'Over here, Matt,' he called and beckoned him with a wave of his right arm.

Matt's forehead was creased with a frown as he made his way across the floor of the emporium, barely touching his hat in the conventional manner to two lady customers being served with a measurement of linen. His son couldn't fail to notice his ruffled feathers. 'What did Doc Hames say?' Jess asked.

'He wasn't there. Out of town at the Coulter ranch. His daughter said she expected him back shortly but I decided not to wait.'

'Anne Hames!' Lars smiled. 'Nice girl. Very pleasant.'

'Uppity, I'd say,' said Matt Clarke. That got the attention of his son and the storekeeper. Both looked to him for further explanation. 'Two weeks, Mr Clarke, she said. Your arm has been in that sling for only two weeks. My father said at least four and he wouldn't say that without meaning it. You can wait and speak to him if you so wish but he won't tell you anything different. It needs to heal properly or it won't heal at all.' He glowered at Lars Freidrikson. 'How does she know how my arm feels. I know it's almost as good as new. Speaking to me like she's got a life time of experience behind her.'

Jess grinned at his father's indignation then addressed himself to Lars Freidrikson. 'Guess her pa taught her the right things to say just like mine taught me.'

Lars chuckled. 'You can't argue with that, Matt. You'll

have to be an invalid for a few more weeks.'

Matt Clarke bridled at his son's teasing but quickly recognized the truth of the storekeeper's words. There wasn't any sensible argument against what Jess had said so, with mock grumping, he set to, as best he was able, loading their supplies onto the flat wagon.

Because of the snow, the emporium emptied quickly. The townswomen with more modest baskets to fill were as anxious to get home as the homesteaders who had arrived with buckboards. Outside, the heavy clouds totally obliterated the natural light, giving a sense of midnight to the late afternoon. Inside, where the paraffin lamps gave a soft, noxious glow, the Clarkes were the last remaining customers. Their task was almost done when raised voices from the adjoining barroom permeated the thin timber of the dividing wall. Lars Freidrikson put down the sack of canned goods he'd intended taking out to Matt Clarke's wagon and rubbed his hands on the bottom of his apron. His wife paused in her addition of the figures in the sales book and looked first in the direction of the disturbance and then at her husband. 'Not again,' Lars murmured as he started towards the door which separated the rooms.

Matt Clarke, standing near the desk where Mrs Freidrikson reckoned his bill, queried the commotion.

'Three times this week,' said Birgid, her voice low but full of concern.

'Who is it?' Matt asked.

'I don't know him.' Birgid spoke with a heavy Swedish accent. She watched her husband pass through the doorway. 'A stranger in town,' she told Matt, 'he confronts Mr Bradall. Someone must stop it. There will be guns.'

Matt crossed the room to follow Lars through to the barroom, and Jess, no less curious than his pa, followed on behind.

Brigg Hutton, the barman, was standing at the end of the counter as though planning on going somewhere, probably into the storehouse to get Lars. Six other men were in the room, five seated around a table near the street door and the other, the one whose voice had brought Lars and the Clarkes to the intersecting door, stood midway between the counter and the table. His left arm was extended, pointing directly at one of the men at the table. His right arm was bent so that his hand hovered inches from the butt of a pistol that he carried in the holster attached to the cartridge belt around his waist.

'You're a murderer, Tim Bradall.' The speaker's face was white, drawn, etched with hatred and determination. 'You killed my sister and I'm going to kill you.' Four of those gathered at the table pushed back their chairs. The fifth sat unmoving, staring at his cards, his head slightly bowed. 'Get up,' yelled the challenger.

'That's enough,' snapped Lars Freidrikson. 'No one fights in here. You want to shout then go into the street.' He looked across at Brigg Hutton and moved his head in a slight nod. Understanding the signal, Brigg produced a shotgun from a shelf under the bar and rested the barrels on the counter. 'Families come here,' Lars continued. 'Nobody fights.'

The man paused a moment then smirked as he spoke

to Lars. 'If nobody fights then it means your man over there isn't going to pull the trigger.' He let his right hand inch closer to his pistol, his neck twisting so that once more he was looking at Tim Bradall.

'Brigg Hutton might not pull the trigger,' said a voice from the street door, 'but if your hand gets any closer to that weapon I will.' The voice was deep and heavy with authority. It was a voice you ignored at your peril.

The man recognized it and the tension in his shoulders eased instantly. 'Sheriff Graydon,' he said.

'Unfasten that gunbelt,' ordered the lawman. 'Let it fall to the ground then walk over here.' The man obeyed but his eyes never left Tim Bradall. They transmitted a message: this time you've survived but there will be other occasions.

Sheriff Graydon, his rifle pointing at the other's chest, spoke again. 'I told you I didn't want any trouble in this town. This is the last time, Hadley. I want you out of Wicker by noon tomorrow.'

Hadley looked past the sheriff, at the snow that was now falling steadily onto the street outside. 'That might be difficult,' he said.

'Stick to the low trails. Route east to Billings or north to Canada will still be passable.'

'Besides,' added Hadley as though the lawman hadn't spoken, 'I've got one of those new repeating rifles ordered. Paid for it, too. Ain't that right, Mr Freidrikson?'

Lars nodded. 'Should have been here by now. When my wagons return it will be among the stock.'

'If it's not here by noon tomorrow Mr Freidrikson will

give you back your money.'

Lars Freidrikson was one of the most cheerful men in Wicker but he was also a businessman and the possible loss of a sale wasn't a recommended way to get on his good side. Especially when the sale was a high profit item like a new Winchester repeating rifle. However, a peaceful life was more important to the Swede than a few extra dollars in the till and if losing a sale was the price to pay to get the man Hadley out of town then he was prepared to do so.

'What's all the trouble about?' Matt Clarke quietly asked Lars.

'That man, Hadley, came to town five days ago. He is telling everyone that Mr Bradall is a murderer, that he has followed him from Arizona to avenge the death of his sister who was Mr Bradall's wife.'

'What does Bradall say?'

'Nothing. Except that he didn't kill his wife. He says he doesn't know where she is.'

'Has he come to Montana to look for her?'

Lars shook his head. 'He's riding for the Triple C. Doesn't say a lot and isn't interested in fighting Hadley. But Hadley is sure pushing for a fight. Lot of people wondering why Mr Bradall hasn't stood up to him.'

'Yeah, and one of them will end up dead when he does.'

Lars shrugged in acceptance of a violent outcome. 'That is what my wife says. I tell her that that is the way it is done in America.' He turned and passed back through the door into the storeroom. At the same time, through the street door into the storeroom, staggered a group of men. Between them, the front two half carried, half dragged a third person and behind them came another two.

'Quickly, Lars,' shouted one of the front men, 'it's Harv.'

'Harv,' repeated Lars in a disbelieving tone. 'What's the matter? What's happened?'

'We found him down by the livery stable. Get him some whiskey. He's near exhausted and frozen.'

This time the excitement in the emporium attracted the attention of the men in the barroom and soon everyone who had witnessed the confrontations between Hadley and Bradall then Hadley and the sheriff were now clustered around the barely conscious form of Harv Prescott, one of the wagon men employed by Lars.

Mrs Freidrikson brought coffee, piping hot, which brought instant pain to Harv as it settled through his system. Food was brought, bread and cheese at first, while the Freidriksons' eldest girl cooked up a skillet of eggs and ham. They threw blankets around him, removed his boots and socks and placed his feet in water just hot enough to gradually increase his body temperature.

'What happened to my wagons?' To some of those gathered around the seated, shivering figure, the storekeeper's blunt inquiry seemed born of self-interest. However, Lars was not a man without empathy, merely a man whose mastery of the English language was not always sufficient to convey the true meaning of his words. As he bent over Harv Prescott what he could read in the man's almost manic stare was a desperate desire to tell his story, to deliver the message he'd fought the elements to bring to Wicker.

Slowly, the details emerged. The convoy that had left Butte four days earlier comprised six wagons. In addition to the two freight wagons belonging to Lars there were three families whose attempt to cross the Rockies into Oregon had been prevented by the sudden winter snow. Travelling further west had become impossible. They'd turned back before getting too high into the mountains and were seeking a friendly settlement where they could wait out the months until spring made the route passable again. Learning of Harv's imminent departure they'd asked to travel with him down to the valley of the Dearborn both for guidance out of the hill country and in the hope that Wicker would provide a welcome for them in their time of need.

The sixth vehicle was an enclosed coach carrying a troupe of dance hall girls en route to the newly opened Red Garter Saloon. Unlike the barroom attached to the emporium which had been established to provide nothing more than a location for ranch-hands and town workers to meet and drink liquor, the Red Garter was designed to separate those same people from their money. It was a big building with a barroom at the front complete with faro tables and a roulette wheel, and behind was a function room with a small stage. Stairs led to a balcony which ran around two sides of the room and off which were several bedrooms. The impresario was Duke Ferris who had opened several saloons of this type in mining towns and cattle towns across the west, making money while the community flourished, but moving on before the mineral petered out or the railway arrived in the area to change the focal point for the cattlemen.

So the six laden wagons had travelled together, slowly, carefully, for the threat of snow had been evident before they left Butte. It began to fall heavily when they were in the high country. Within hours the trail was almost obliterated. The iron rimmed wheels struggled to gain purchase in the snow and the horses slipped and collided with each other as they were urged to haul their loads up hill or as they were restrained in the long descents towards the valley. Blizzards and squalls enforced many stops and, at some places where the snow had drifted and the route became unrecognizable to the teamsters, it became necessary to lead the horses both for encouragement of the beasts and to ensure that no landmarks were missed as the falling snow confused their vision. The snow hid a multitude of obstacles. Rocks and fallen branches lay beneath an even, white blanket, giving the drivers and their companions no opportunity to relax their vigil. The snow fell harder, the wind blew stronger and the temperature dropped lower.

What had begun as a three day journey was at the end of its fourth day when they reached the descent into Two Falls Pass. This was the last stretch in the high country and the teamsters were aware that once they'd made it through the Pass they would be in the valley of the Dearborn with Wicker a six hour drive away. Although they knew that in the current conditions they were unlikely to reach Wicker before nightfall next day, there was a spirit of achievement among the travellers as they made camp that night. The snow had been lighter on the eastern side of the hills and when they arose next morning it wasn't falling at all.

Then, suddenly, disaster struck. They had just got underway again when an avalanche of snow came sliding down the mountainside. No one knew how it started. It was almost upon them before the noise of the sliding snow and ice was recognized. Alerted by the cracking of tumbling trees, it was a lad from one of the families back in the line who hollered the first warning. But his voice was still soft, not much deeper than a girl's, and it barely carried to the wagon in front. Precious seconds were lost as each wagon shouted to the driver ahead but the warning came too late for the leading freight wagon. The great gush of snow swept it from the trail without an audible shout from the men, or whinny from the horses, or rattle of destruction from the wagon as its wheels broke, its sides splintered and its contents were shed into the gorge below.

The other wagons had slithered to a halt. Harv Prescott, driving the second freight wagon, had turned his team into the side of the mountain, below a huge outcrop, which had, to a great extent, deflected the falling snow beyond his horses and wagon. The startled beasts lunged and kicked and while Harv held tightly to the leathers to prevent them taking flight, Cal Brewster, his sidekick, had jumped down from the driving board to grab the bridles of the lead pair. He talked to them in an effort to keep them calm while the frozen debris fell beyond them and continued on its drive down to the floor of the valley below.

The avalanche lasted no more than two minutes but

such was the noise and force of the slide while it lasted that Harv Prescott couldn't believe that no harm had come to himself, Cal or any of the four horses attached to the wagon. The overhang had saved them from the same fate that had befallen their colleagues but, even so, Cal, who had retained his grip on the horses throughout, was waist deep in snow. The trail ahead had been rendered impassable for the wagons. An array of timber and ice blocks had been left behind by the avalanche and would have to be cleared away before the party could progress to Wicker.

Leaving Cal to pacify the animals, Harv had gone back along the line to assess the damage to the other wagons. Fortunately they hadn't all been in the path of the avalanche but, even so, the two wagons directly behind him had collided when one startled team became too much for the inexperienced teamster to hold. In the ensuing jumble, horses skidded and tumbled, were trod upon and kicked, legs were broken and internal injuries sustained. Three had to be destroyed. In addition, both vehicles had broken wheels and one of them also had a damaged shaft. But it wasn't just the wagons and animals that had suffered damage. The people inside had been thrown about. One man had a broken arm and another, whose face was etched with agony with each breath he took, was diagnosed with broken ribs. He'd been crushed under a falling horse whilst trying to calm his team in the melee. A woman had taken a severe blow to the head and was unconscious. Several others had cuts and bruises.

A hasty meeting agreed that someone had to go for

help. Even if the wagons could be repaired, there weren't sufficient able bodied men in the party to clear a passage for them. Some people needed medical treatment but there weren't enough horses for everyone to ride on to Wicker. Harv volunteered to go on alone, using a makeshift rope bridle and nothing more than a rough blanket over the wagon horse's back. He estimated he would reach Wicker that night and would have rescuers back before nightfall the next day. A mountain lion altered the timetable.

The snow began to fall again when Harv was a mere half-hour away from the wagons. For ten minutes it swirled around him so hard that he could barely see beyond the head of his horse. He wanted to stop, wait out the snow storm because in such conditions it would be easy to miss the trail, plunge into a snowdrift or even slip off the mountain. But the people back up the mountain were depending on him so he kept going, concentrating on sitting easily on the horse, keeping it calm because he knew that it would react if it sensed his own unease. At first it picked its feet high with every step but, when the snow stopped and they were near the foot of the mountain, it was apparent that there was less snow on the ground. That's when Harv's vigilance slipped. He didn't see the mountain lion until he was passing the ledge on which it lay, and its scent hadn't carried to his mount until the same moment.

The cat squealed. The horse snorted and reared and, without a saddle, Harv slipped off its back and landed awkwardly on the ground. With the breath knocked out of him he needed a moment to gather his wits. The raucous sounds of fighting animals swiftly penetrated his fuzzy brain and he staggered to his feet. The cat was lying along the horse's neck, it's teeth sinking into the soft underflesh. The horse shrieked, no natural sound for a horse, no sound that Harv had ever before heard from a horse or any other animal. He drew his six-gun and aimed at the cat. At that moment his horse shook its head and Harv couldn't fire lest he hit the wrong animal. Twice more he took aim but the safety of his own frantic animal prevented him from pulling the trigger.

Then the horse jumped and stamped, like a rodeo bronco trying to unseat a rider, and the cat loosened its grip on its throat. Harv fired, hitting the mountain lion in the back. It squealed and fell to the ground. Harv ran forward three steps and fired again, this time hitting the cat in the back of the head. It flopped on its side and, with a sense of relief that the cat had attacked the horse rather than himself, Harv put another bullet in its head to make sure it was dead.

The horse was wild-eyed, alternatively snorting to regain its breath and emitting a high-pitched whine to register its pain and fear. As Harv approached, its front legs buckled and it sank to its knees. Harv could see streaks of blood on its neck and hoped they were from the wounds he'd inflicted on the mountain lion but knew they were not. When he got closer he could see a black hole in the snow, a hole created by the blood that was pouring from the animal's punctured throat. If it died it would leave him afoot. Self-preservation urged him to entice the horse to its feet but he could see that it was in pain and dying. He drew his gun again and shot it.

A bitter wind blew as he put fresh shells into the revolver. He shivered. There was a long walk ahead and he wasn't sure he would complete it.

He'd walked for almost twenty-four hours, afraid to stop lest he fell asleep, knowing that if he fell asleep he would never wake up, and if he died then so, too, would those stranded on the mountain.

'You've got to get to those people,' Harv implored those gathered around. 'They need help. They need a doctor.'

Sheriff Graydon took charge, issuing orders to one man to get Doc Hames and scanning the faces of the people standing around to see who would be suitable to join him in a rescue party.

'I have no more employees,' declared Lars Freidrikson. 'Harv cannot go back and Cal is already up there. Buck and Totem,' he added, mentioning the men who had driven the other freight wagon, his tone heavy with remorse, 'will not come back.'

Matt Clarke was next to speak. 'If you think I can be of use, Sheriff, I'll go with you.'

Sheriff Graydon shook his head. 'No, Matt. It'll be heavy work up there. There'll be other men about town who'll go.'

'Hurd Baker and the Flynn boys were here earlier,' Matt said. 'They'd have joined your rescue party.'

'True, but I can't wait for someone bringing them back from their spreads. Those people have been stuck up in the Bitterroots for two days. The weather conditions will have been a lot worse for them than they have been for us. We need to get to them as quickly as possible. I'd like to get underway within the hour.' He looked around the room once more. 'So who'll come with me?'

Dan Hathaway was the first to volunteer. No one knew the territory around Wicker better than Dan who, in his younger days, had trapped animals and mined for minerals both sides of the Bitterroot range. These days he hired himself out wherever there was work to do and wages to be paid. Sometimes he was fixing fences on a farm, sometimes he was hauling freight and sometimes he was herding cattle to a railhead. No one, including himself, knew for sure how old he was but everyone knew he was as strong as any other man in town and, coupled with his survival skills, that strength was enough to earn him respect wherever he went. 'I'll gather my gear,' he told Sheriff Graydon, 'and meet y'all at the stables.'

When he'd gone, Sheriff Graydon spoke again, laying out his plan, trying not to dramatize the task ahead in such a way that would deter men from volunteering. 'Six willing men should be enough,' he said. 'Good men, like Dan. I'll take Rory with me,' he said, referring to his deputy, Rory Blades. 'So I just need another three. We'll need to take spare horses to bring those people down from the mountain and we'll use them to carry up ropes and digging implements. We should reach Two Falls Pass tonight. We'll camp there and begin the climb in daylight. With luck we'll have them back here in two days.'

Tim Bradall pushed a hand through his fair hair. 'I suppose the Triple C will get by without me for a couple of days. I'll go with you, Sheriff.'

Sheriff Graydon nodded, appreciative of the recent arrival's desire to lend a hand at this hour of need. But he was less pleased when the next volunteer spoke up.

'Reckon I'll go, too, Sheriff,' said Reub Hadley, a thin smile on his long face.

'That's not a good idea,' said Graydon. 'We need men who'll work together. This trip will be no place for carrying personal quarrels.'

'Just trying to obey your order, Sheriff. You said you wanted me out of Wicker by noon tomorrow and I'm proposing to do just that. Besides, I've got another reason for going along. My new Winchester is stuck up on that mountain.'

Sheriff Graydon looked from Reub Hadley to Tim Bradall and back again. Reub Hadley retained the thin smile that the sheriff didn't trust. Tim Bradall met his gaze with unblinking eyes. 'Hadley, this is the only warning you'll get. If you pursue this vendetta, if you endanger our efforts to save those people trapped on the mountain, I'll shoot you dead.'

Hadley's lips stretched further, his eyes narrowed, too. 'Just trying to be a good citizen, Sheriff.'

'That's five then,' said Graydon.

Jess Clarke spoke. 'I'll be the sixth,' he said.

'Jess,' his father said, surprise at his son's declaration almost eliciting an instant refusal.

'You can't go, Pa,' said Jess, 'but you'd do it in an instant if your arm was good, and you'd do it because you'd believe it to be the right thing to do. Got to help our neighbours, you'd say. Well we'll still be helping them except it'll be me going up there instead of you.'

'But what about our wagon?' Matt didn't care about the wagon. He knew he could drive it home with one arm. The team could find its way home without him and, in a blizzard such as the one which was blowing at that moment, they would be going slow enough for a Boston parson to drive. It was Mary he was thinking of, and what he would tell her.

'I'll unload it when I get back,' said Jess. To Sheriff Graydon he said, 'I'm strong enough, Sheriff. I won't let you down.'

'You haven't got a horse,' said his father.

'We'll have to take some from Seb's livery,' said the sheriff. 'The town'll pay for the hire.'

Matt couldn't find another argument. For his mother's sake he wanted to prevent Jess going, but beneath his own apprehension he realized that his son was now man enough to make his own decisions. 'Here,' he said. He pulled out the old double action revolver he carried tucked into the waistband of his trousers. 'You'd better take this. There may be more mountain lions up there.'

Jess took the gun, looked at it with surprise, for rarely did his father allow him to fire it and never before without his supervision. For a moment he considered refusing it but one look at his father's face told him that this was a moment of significance, a gesture of trust and worthiness. He slipped it into the inside pocket of his long winter coat feeling inches taller, inches broader.

So it was settled that the rescue party would consist of Sheriff Graydon, his deputy, Rory Blades, Tim Bradall, Reub Hadley, Dan Hathaway and Jess Clarke. In addition, Doc Hames would go along to provide the necessary medical care. Although he had still not been at

41

home when the sheriff's message had been delivered, his daughter had assured the messenger that he would be with them when they were ready to leave.

Preparations were well under way and the group were assembled at the livery stable when Cy Tranter who ran the telegraph office rushed among them waving a piece of paper. 'Sheriff,' he called, 'I'm pleased I've caught you. Telegram from Missoula. Urgent.'

Sheriff Graydon took the offered sheet and read it. 'The bank's been robbed,' he said. 'Looks like the work of the Claytons and they've killed two people making their getaway. Sheriff Martin suspects they're heading towards Wicker.' He folded the sheet and tucked it in a pocket. 'Reckon that means I can't go with you,' he told the assembled riders. 'I'll have to stay here to make sure they don't try to attack this town. Rory, you'll be in charge but listen to Dan if he offers advice. He knows the mountains better than any other man.'

'Well,' said Dan, 'if you're gonna listen to my advice I'd say that we're going to be one man light if you don't go, Sheriff. I know the doc's coming along but he ain't exactly the mightiest man I've ever come across so I suggest we find somebody else quick. Better to take a few more minutes now than fail in our quest later.'

'What about Duke Ferris?' said Rory. 'He's got a stake in those people trapped on the mountain, ain't he?'

'He does,' murmured Sheriff Graydon but he couldn't see Duke Ferris risking his own hide to rescue other people and the men he employed were not from the mould of solid citizens. Still, time was of the essence and a general plea for assistance within the Red Garter might prove fruitful.

In fact, Duke Ferris was concerned by the news that his troupe of dance hall girls was stranded in the Bitterroots. He'd spent a lot of money on the Red Garter and he wasn't going to get it back by selling whiskey alone. He needed those girls to separate his customers from their money and if this group didn't get through then there wouldn't be any chance of any others getting through before spring. So he sent his trouble-shooter to join the rescue party, an unlikely choice because Clay Brascoe's reputation wasn't with a spade or pick but with a gun. Taking orders from a deputy sheriff would be contrary to his known history. But when he arrived it was without any show of antipathy to what had to be done. He stood at the back of the group, apparently listening to the sheriff's instructions as avidly as any other man there.

Finally, in the livery stable, they mounted, six men each leading another mount some of which were loaded with tools and equipment they expected to need. They moved out when Doc Hames arrived, a slight figure huddled inside the blue winter campaign coat of his earlier army career, its collar turned up high to stave off the cold to his neck and his wide-brimmed hat pulled down tight for extra protection. Matt Clarke, who had stayed in town until the departure of the rescue group, muttered a brief, 'Good luck,' as he watched the seven ride off into the snow, gone from sight before they had taken a dozen strides beyond the town limits.

CHAPTER TWO

Progress was slow. The horses went forward without eagerness, reduced to walking pace as the heavy snow came at them from the high ground that was their destination. The initial darkness of a snow filled sky eventually gave way to the natural blackness at the onset of a winter evening. By the time they'd covered five miles, the snow, which had been nothing more than a covering of Wicker's main street, was hock high, deadening the sound of hoof beats and lending an eerie atmosphere to their advance. The wind blew in icy gusts.

The group of seven rode in close formation. Dan Hathaway and Rory Blades led the way with Hadley, Brascoe and Bradall in a line behind. Jess rode at the rear with Doc Hames. No-one spoke, everyone seeking the protection of their winter coats, gloves and hats. Chins were tucked against chests as the frequent chill blasts battered against any exposed parts, which, for most riders, was their eyes. Only Jess Clarke rode without the lower part of his face covered.

Although the hat he wore had been sensible enough for the journey into town to collect the stores, it was now

44

a matter of regret. Out in the wilderness it was unsuitable. True, the one he wore had side pieces to protect his ears but it was small, offering no protection at all to the back of his head. Even with the collar of his thick winter coat turned up there was a portion of his head that was covered only by his hair and the wool scarf his mother had draped around his neck before leaving home. He hunched his shoulders in an effort to close the gap between collar and cap, but to no avail. The wind seemed to be trapped there and the more his thoughts lingered on the coldness of his neck the more the coldness seemed to spread over the rest of his head. He looked across at Doc Hames. The doctor seemed to be having the opposite problem. His leather plains hat seemed to be too large for his head. It was low on his brow but the wide brim which overlapped the collar of his long, campaign coat seemed to present a problem of its own. Doc Hames was continuously placing a hand on the crown as though the wind was getting under the brim and about to blow it away. Jess couldn't help thinking that the doctor was wearing a hat that was too big for him, as though he'd picked up someone else's hat in his hurry to join up with the rescue party.

The plan was to follow the river along the valley to Two Falls Pass before making camp for the night. Although they'd brought with them the means to manufacture fire brands to light their way, it was generally agreed that they would be better waiting until daylight to tackle the high ground. Besides, the horses needed rest as much as the men. In normal conditions, without asking too much of a horse, this stage could be completed in four hours, but these weren't normal conditions. Already they'd been travelling more than five hours and were still several miles from Two Falls Pass.

Snow was no longer falling when Rory Blades raised his hand to bring the party to a halt. They gathered in a tight ring, the mingled breath from the horses rising like steam from an invisible cauldron. The deputy lowered the scarf from around his mouth so that his voice could be heard when he explained his strategy. 'It'll be another two hours before we get to the Pass but we'll stick to the plan. The horses are able to go on at this pace for a deal of time yet. Dan tells me that when we get to the Pass there are caves we can shelter in for the night and we'll be able to build a fire. For now, chew a bit of jerky while we ride.' He looked at everyone in the party, gave them a chance to voice an opinion or ask a question, but no-one did. He turned his horse and started off into the darkness again, Dan Hathaway going with him and Hadley, Brascoe and Bradall with their spare horses, following behind.

Jess turned his horse. Like the other riders, he had the long lead of his pack horse tied around the saddle horn which kept it close by and his hands free. Nonetheless, he gave the lead a tug at the same time as he set his heels to the horse beneath him so that both animals moved off together. He hadn't taken more than two strides when a sound, a cry of exasperation, came to him from behind. He looked over his shoulder and saw that the spare horse being led by Doc Hames had somehow wandered to the wrong side of the doctor's mount. As a consequence, the long lead attached to the saddle horn was wrapped around the doctor. To untangle himself, the doctor was now trying to turn the horse he was astride so that he could bring it around behind the pack animal and restore it once again to his right hand side. But the foreshortened rein made such a manoeuvre difficult. The pack horse, confused by the orders of the tightened rein, became skittish, wouldn't stay still for the doctor to ride around it. Then the doctor's mount slipped and bumped against the pack animal and in the ensuing scramble, Doc Hames was dislodged from the saddle and fell into the snow between the two horses.

Fearing for the doctor's safety, Jess leapt down from his saddle, dragged the reins over his horse's head and dropped them to the ground. The livery horse would, he figured, be well enough schooled to think itself tethered when the reins were in that position, and the pack horse wouldn't move until urged to do so by the line attached to its bridle. The other animals had moved some distance away from the figure that lay face down in the snow and, although the reins were not yet untangled, both horses seemed calm and resigned to wait for further instruction.

Snow had fallen heavily at this end of the valley and had drifted off the open plain so that at this place it was knee deep. Jess knelt beside Doc Hames, put his hand on his shoulders and tried to raise his head from the deep depression it had formed. A moan escaped from behind the scarf that covered the mouth. At least, Jess thought, the doctor was alive. However, he needed to turn him over, needed to get his head out of the grave-like depression he'd formed.

The doctor stirred as Jess worked his hands under the arms, shuffling the body from side to side until they were around the chest. Then he pulled, lifting the weight, intending to drag the doctor up and over so that he could get air into his lungs. But no sooner had he begun lifting than he felt the body beneath him stiffen, as though recoiling from his touch, and the sounds coming from the mouth were those of protest, outrage, and the man began moving of his own volition, turning, arms pushing Jess away like he was an enemy, someone to fear. But it wasn't just the reaction of the doctor that startled Jess. Subconsciously, things had registered in his mind, subtle warnings that what he was dealing with was not what he thought he was dealing with. First, even though Doctor Hames was a slight man, he seemed surprisingly easy to lift, then, when he'd got his hands underneath and clutched the chest, the sensation had been totally unexpected. Even as his mind was trying to tell him that the pliant mass beneath his hands was due to the sub-stance of the doctor's army greatcoat or his own gloves, he knew well enough that it was not. Now, as he stumbled back from the thrusting arms, instead of the bushy, greyish eyebrows of Doc Hames, he saw fine, arched eye-brows over blazing, youthful eyes, and from beneath the dislodged wide plains hat, wisps and strands of long, light brown hair.

'Anne,' he said. 'Anne Hames. What are you doing here?'

Her eyes were big, showing a startled expression, a mixture of indignation and fear, but the fear dwindled as she recognized Jess Clarke. She shuffled inside her father's greatcoat then, in agitated fashion, pushed the loose hair back under her hat. The significance of that act was not lost on Jess as he recalled how often she'd struggled to keep the hat in place during the ride. It seemed a forlorn hope if she thought she could keep her identity a secret. 'What are you doing here?' he asked again.

Anne Hames snapped an answer at Jess, her testiness less a show of anger, more an attempt to disguise the embarrassment of her discovery. 'I should have thought it was obvious what I'm doing here. Someone is needed to provide medical aid to the people trapped by the avalanche and my father wasn't available.'

'But Anne,' Jess said, and he hesitated because although her eyes were the only part of her face he could see, he had never before noticed how bright they were and brown like polished shells of hazel nuts. Even in the darkness of the night he was captivated by their colour. 'You're not a doctor,' he concluded.

'I've attended my father's patients with him for several years. I know what to look for and how to treat most wounds.'

'Some of the injured have broken bones,' Jess told her. 'Can you help them?'

Her eyelids lowered, a momentary display of doubt. 'I'll do what I can,' she stubbornly declared. 'Better they get what help I can give than none at all.'

'What about your father? Why didn't he come?'

'He hadn't returned from the Coulters' place. Sheriff Graydon was anxious to get underway and I didn't want to delay him. When the rest of the party was ready I tagged along. I figured as long as I got to Two Falls Pass without being discovered they wouldn't send me back.'

Jess looked up at the sky from where large flakes of snow were beginning to fall again. 'I don't reckon anyone will send you back now. You couldn't go alone and the party isn't big enough to spare anyone to go with you.'

'Still,' she said softly, as though asking for his complicity in her plan, 'I'd rather they didn't know until we got to the pass.'

'I'd rather they didn't know at all. It ain't right, you the only girl.'

'I won't be when we reach the stranded families,' she said.

Jess acknowledged the truth of that statement but it didn't cheer him. Still, this wasn't the time to argue. 'You're right,' he said. 'We just have to keep your identity secret until tomorrow. Now,' he added, 'we need to catch up to the others before this new snow covers their trail.'

They rounded up their horses and Jess retied the lead rein of Anne's pack horse to her saddle horn so that it wasn't long enough for it to pass behind her mount again. As she prepared to climb into the saddle the wind once again played with her hat and she planted her hand on the crown to stop it blowing away.

Jess unwound the scarf his mother had given him from around his neck. 'Here,' he said, reaching across to Anne and tying the scarf under her chin so that it secured the hat to her head and provided covering for her ears. Although he had no obvious cause to suspect that her discovery would place her in any danger from the other men in the party, he was still prepared to have the back of his own head more exposed to the elements than to have them know her identity before they started up the mountain in the morning. After all, two of the group had been perilously close to violence against each other only moments before the plight of the travellers had been divulged, and that argument had been about a woman. Also, there was Clay Brascoe. He'd arrived in town with a violent reputation – a man quick to use his fists and his gun. In the eyes of the citizens of Wicker, that reputation had been enhanced when he'd gone to work for Duke Ferris, backing his plans to bring gambling tables and prostitution to the Red Garter. Jess was holding the bridle of her saddle horse, waiting for her to mount, when, out of the night, a rider slowly approached. The long, fringed, buckskin coat and tailed coonskin hat made the man easily identifiable. 'What's keeping you?' yelled Dan Hathaway when he was still twenty yards away.

'Horses got entangled,' explained Jess. 'All sorted now,' he added and nodded to Anne, a gesture which acted as a signal for her get astride the horse and for Dan Hathaway to rein his own horse to a halt while he waited for them to join him. When Anne was mounted, Jess released his hold on the bridle and stepped across to his own horse. 'Let's go,' he said when he, too, was in the saddle, and began following the tracks of those that had gone before. When he passed Dan Hathaway he couldn't fail to see the suspicious look in the older man's eyes.

Everyone was grateful for the respite from the driving snow when they eventually reached the cave that Dan

Hathaway had predicted was most suitable for their purpose. There were, Dan had told Rory Blades, abandoned cabins that would provide better, warmer shelter for the night but they were higher up the mountain and he reckoned the horses deserved a rest before tackling the high ground. The entrance was large; no one using it had to stoop, but, because of the presence of two large boulders in critical positions, its existence wasn't obvious from the trail. Once inside, the gallery veered to the right providing an element of protection from the cold and wind outside, and then it divided into two separate caverns, one of which they used as a stall for the horses.

At first, the horses were reluctant to go into the cave, shying in the entrance way, rearing and pulling back, eyes rolling as they snorted their alarm.

'Cats,' declared Dan. 'Place has been used by mountain lions. Their scent is still obvious. The horses are scared.'

'Do you think there are any in there now?' Deputy Blades tried to peer into the darkness of the mountainside as he asked the question.

Dan shook his head. 'Smell ain't that strong. They're acting up because they're already skittered by the snow.' He pulled his own mount into the cave and once inside, in the darkness and dependent upon Dan's guidance, it settled and went where it was led. With one inside, the others followed easily.

From a sack on his pack animal, Rory produced a couple of prepared torches, thick, green sticks with a wad of cloth wrapped around one end, and a can of cooking oil. He carried them back towards the entrance, into the modicum of light it provided and away from the horses. Dousing the cloth with oil, the deputy lit the torches with a match and carried them back to the rest of the party.

'Lars Freidrikson says that these give about thirty minutes of light,' he told everyone. 'That should be enough time to get the horses unsaddled and unpacked.'

Dan Hathaway took one of the torches and jammed it into a crevice in the back wall so that most of its light was shed into the cavern where the horses were stabled but a little of it cast a glow in the main chamber. Tim Bradall, who had taken the other torch from the deputy, needed to pack loose rubble around it to keep it upright between two rocks. Between them, the two torches didn't provide sufficient light to light up the whole of the cave or to distinguish one person from another, but Deputy Blades refused to light more. He'd brought a dozen, insufficient to use up recklessly and conscious of the storekeeper's caution that it was seldom worth extinguishing them part spent. He delved into the pockets below his heavy topcoat and brought out a timepiece that looked many years older than him. 'Midnight,' he declared. 'I figure on five hours' rest. We'll be sleeping most of that time and we won't need light then. Besides, there's kindling among the supplies so if someone wants to set about getting a fire going that'll throw a bit more light and we can have hot coffee before we turn in.'

Reub Hadley was the only one who voiced any opposition to the scheme. 'Knowing we have a killer among us I'd as soon we had as much light as possible. Wouldn't want someone taking advantage of the dark to put a knife in me while I'm sleeping.'

Clay Brascoe, suspecting that Hadley referred to him, turned a cold eye towards the speaker. But Hadley was staring at Tim Bradall who, in response, was shuffling inside his coat as though trying to make himself as small as possible, trying to deflect Hadley's accusation away from himself. Remembering the account he'd heard of their confrontation a couple of days earlier, Brascoe grinned. There was nothing he liked more than the threat of violence and when it was caused by something as meaningless as a woman it amused him even more.

'No one is going to kill anyone,' said Rory Blades, trying to stamp his authority on the group. 'We're up here to save lives so I don't want any more talk of that kind.'

Tim Bradall had, by this time, turned his back on the group and was heading towards the horses.

'Doc,' said Dan Hathaway, 'if you start on the fire me and Jess'll take care of your animals.' Anne Hames lifted her head slightly, as though about to voice a protest, but Jess Clarke, who was standing by her side, spoke to her in a low voice. 'That would seem to be the best thing to do, don't you think?' The flash of anger in Anne's eyes showed her desire to disagree, to argue that she was as capable of lifting down a saddle as he was, but recognition of the need to remain incognito until they were with the wagon people tempered her response. She could see that the more she kept apart from the others the less likely the chance of discovery. Reluctantly, she nodded her head.

Dan Hathaway knew of a depression in the cave floor in which to build a fire. He'd used it in the past. It was near the right hand wall and as free from draught as any point in a cave is ever likely to be. By the time the horses had been unloaded Anne had packed the dry kindling into the hole and got a fire lit. And, too, she'd filled Rory's coffee pot with beans and fresh snow and had it heating in the flames.

No one had removed any clothing since entering the cave; Anne still had the scarf around her head that was keeping her hat in place, and the neckerchief covering the lower half of her face. When the coffee was brewed everyone sat around in a half circle facing the fire. Anne sat at one end, a pace behind everyone else, hoping that no random flicker of a flame would light up her face. Fate was with her, an outburst of violence ensured that she was not the focus of attention.

Rory Blades did most of the talking while they drank coffee and chewed some dried beef. Harv Prescott, he told them, hadn't been able to give the precise location of the stranded travellers so there was no way of telling how long it would take to reach them. All they knew for sure was that they were somewhere on the regular trail but even that didn't make finding them a simple matter because so much snow had fallen that the trail would be difficult to define. That being so, he concluded, because of Dan Hathaway's knowledge of the Bitterroots, when they set out in the morning, it would be Dan who made the decisions and gave the orders.

When the deputy stopped talking the only sounds within the cave were the crackling of the burning twigs and the occasional scraping of metal on stone from the horses in the other chamber. Jess glanced over his shoulder at Anne Hames but all he saw was the crown of her wide hat. She sat cross legged, tin coffee cup gripped between her gloved hands, shoulders stooped so that her chin almost touched her chest. Although they hadn't exchanged another word since he'd discovered her identity back above the Dearborn, she hadn't been out of his thoughts. The secret of her identity carried with it responsibility which, in turn, aroused in him a sense of protectiveness. He wanted to go to her, speak to her, assure himself of her well-being, but most of all he wanted to see again those brown eyes looking into his own. Suddenly he realized he'd been gazing in her direction far too long. Being over attentive was the surest way of drawing attention to Anne and betraying her identity. He looked at the other men sitting around the fire, all of them, it seemed, intent on chewing or drinking coffee. Only Dan Hathaway looked his way and for the merest moment it seemed as though the old mountain man was giving him a sign, a warning. It was a brief shake of his head, a message in keeping with his own thoughts – don't draw attention to the girl. Did Dan Hathaway know that the person sitting behind the circle wasn't Doc Hames? Did he know it was a girl?

His contemplation of Dan's signal was interrupted by the man sitting next to him. Clay Brascoe spoke, his words seemingly aimed at the flames which lit up his face. 'So,' he began, 'this woman that you two are fighting over, which one of you stole her from the other?'

'Quit it, Brascoe,' said Rory Blades. 'I don't want anyone stirring up trouble. Besides, it's none of our business.'

'Sure it is, Deputy.' Brascoe couldn't withhold the sneer in his tone. He had no respect for lawmen, especially small town lawmen who had no reputation. 'You need to know the story before they kill each other. Then you'll know what to put in your report.' He grinned, an unpleasant, challenging grin.

'Shut up, Brascoe,' said Rory, but at the same time someone else spoke.

Reub Hadley's voice was low but filled with hatred as it had been when he'd confronted Tim Bradall in the barroom of Lars Freidrikson's emporium. 'She's my sister,' he began, 'a bright and beautiful girl raised in Fort Worth by God-fearing parents. Then he came along.' Reub Hadley pointed at Tim Bradall. 'Took her from her family to live in some isolated spot on the Arizona range land.'

In an instant, Tim Bradall was on his feet, leaning forward at the waist, his jaw thrust angrily towards Reub Hadley. 'We were married. Remember? You were at the wedding and just as happy about it as your parents were. We went to Arizona to raise cattle and farm the land like a lot of other people. And, what with the dry land and the unpredictable weather and the disease and the Indians, like a lot of other people we didn't find it easy. Your sister couldn't take any more. She left.' For a few seconds no-one moved, his words echoing around the cave, his anger hovering over them as had the snow clouds in the sky.

Perhaps it would have ended with that outburst if Rory Blades hadn't once again tried to impose his authority. 'Enough said on the subject,' he declared. 'No more talk.

It's time to bed down.'

Reub Hadley threw him a defiant look. No one was going to tell him when to stop talking. 'Where did she go?' his question directed at Tim Bradall.

Imperceptibly, the antagonism in Tim Bradall's posture eased. The tension of his body relaxed, the taut lines around his mouth faded away. 'I've told you before,' he said, 'I don't know.' His voice was softer, less confident and there wasn't a person sitting around the fire who believed him.

'Don't know,' snarled Reub Hadley, 'but you sold up and moved away from Arizona without any warning to your neighbours. Our letters came straight back to us. I've trailed you from place to place for a year but I've never heard one word about Caroline. She didn't leave with you and I reckon you killed her and buried her out on the prairie.'

Silence followed the accusation; Reub Hadley adamant that he'd cornered the man he accused of killing his sister; Tim Bradall losing the drive to argue, withdrawing from confrontation.

'Seems to me,' Clay Brascoe said, his tone implying that he was about to pour oil on troubled water, 'that perhaps our friend here didn't kill your sister. Don't seem likely if the stories I've heard about Arizona farmers is true.'

'Shut up,' snapped Tim Bradall.

'What stories? Reub Hadley asked.

'Hear tell that a wife can be a steady source of income when times are hard.'

'I told you to shut up.' Tim Bradall's face showed a

heat that belied the temperature in the cave.

'What do you mean?' Reub asked, though he'd heard the rumours before as had Rory Blades and Dan Hathaway.

'Cavalry patrol comes by and the soldiers are in need of some, what shall we call it – refreshment. The stables off limits to the horses that day. Heard tell that a good wife can earn a handful of dollars.'

Reub threw a murderous look at Tim Bradall. 'This true? Did you do that to my sister? Sell her to soldiers to pay for your pathetic patch of land?'

'Of course,' intoned Clay Brascoe as though he had never been interrupted, 'there's an even better way of getting rid of an unwanted wife than killing her.' He paused, not looking up, concentrating on the flames flickering from the sticks in the hole, knowing he had everyone's attention, especially Reub Hadley's. If they'd met at any other time Reub Hadley would have had as much in common with Clay Brascoe as a jack rabbit with a rattlesnake; he'd have avoided him and ignored his comments as those of a person inferior in social rank and intellect but, at this moment, in this cave, confronting the man he believed responsible for killing his sister, he was the disciple of anyone whose words were a possible confirmation of his own opinion. The possibility that Clay Brascoe was goading him for his own amusement never occurred to him. 'Trade her to the Comanche,' said Brascoe. 'That way our friend would be telling the truth when he said he didn't know where she was. Could be anywhere between Oklahoma City and the Rio Grande. If she's still alive, that is. And Mr Hadley, I sure hope she ain't. Boy, what those Comanche do to a woman. A fellow told me—'

'That's enough,' said Dan Hathaway, but his attempt to cool down the situation came too late. Reub Hadley had taken Brascoe's bait, his lips were curled away from his teeth and his eyes blazed hatred at the man standing before him.

'Sold my sister to Indians,' he snarled. At the same time as he tried to stand, his gloved hands began to fumble at the buttons of his heavy outer coat, his intention of reaching for a weapon clear for all to see.

The anger bottled up inside Tim Bradall now overflowed. He flung his near empty tin mug at his brother-in-law, hitting him on the bridge of the nose, cutting it, drawing blood. Before Reub could wipe away the smear, Tim's right hand had followed close behind, landing on the other's jaw. It had been an awkward blow, punching down at the still rising Reub, and Tim overbalanced, falling on his opponent in a tangle of arms and legs and a series of grunts and shouts.

All the shouts weren't voiced by the combatants. Everyone had scrambled to their feet to avoid the brawlers. Rory Blades was yelling at them to quit fighting and as the struggle began in earnest he reached for his rifle which he'd propped against the wall, close at hand. He had his finger inside the trigger guard and shuffled from side to side, aiming at one man then the other but unable, or unwilling to shoot at anyone. Eventually, decision made, he pointed the gun in the air but before he could pull the trigger the rifle was pulled from his hands.

'Fire that in here and the slug'll bounce around like a

ball on a pool table,' warned Dan Hathaway. 'Could hit anyone. To say nothing of scaring the horses out of here and leaving us all afoot.' Rory looked abashed. 'Let them fight,' said Dan. 'Nothing you can do to stop them now.'

He was right. The two men on the ground were trading blows as furiously as a lucky prospector trades his dust for a saloon keeper's wares. Tim Bradall's assault had taken Reub Hadley by surprise, consequently he'd taken three blows in addition to the cut from the coffee cup before being able to wrestle himself on top. However, the effectiveness of their punches was significantly hampered by their cumbersome clothing. Not only were they unable to swing their arms freely when delivering a punch, but the many layers also absorbed much of the power behind those which landed on the body. Still, they fought with the sort of intensity expected of a long standing feud. They grunted and cursed, first one holding the upper hand then the other.

It ended after a short right to the jaw sent Reub Hadley sprawling against a wall. Tim Bradall was upon him in a flash, grabbing his hair and banging his head against the stone wall. Bradall attempted another such blow but Reub managed to raise his knees, giving him some leverage between his body and his opponent's. He thrust with his legs, spilling Tim Bradall away from him, rolling him towards the fire. Reub pounced as Tim attempted to get to his feet, charging forward, head lowered, butting Bradall in the stomach. They fell together, Tim on his back, his head in the flames, Reub Hadley on his chest. Despite Tim's yells as his hair singed, Reub held him down, pitilessly watching the other's agony.

Dan Hathaway knelt at Reub's side. 'Let him up.' He spoke quietly, the hunting knife he held against Hadley's throat a louder command than his words. For a moment more Reub Hadley pressed down but a glance at Dan's face and the feel of steel against his skin abated his blood lust.

Rory Blades dragged Tim Bradall away from the fire, dabbing at the smouldering jacket as he did so. 'Doc,' he shouted, 'you got anything to put on these burns?' His voice was loud, too loud, registering his concern that the situation was getting out of hand, that there was going to be trouble that he might not be able to handle. 'Sheriff Graydon told me to shoot either of you that put this expedition in danger and that's just what I'll do.' Sheriff Graydon would have done that, he was a lawman of the old school who followed up what he said with deeds. No-one believed it of Rory Blades, especially Dan Hathaway.

For a moment, Dan considered his fellow travellers – a deputy sheriff whose expectation of wielding authority was a naive hope; brothers-in-law so consumed with hatred for each other that they were a handicap to the whole rescue attempt; Clay Brascoe, a gunslinger, as out of place as an angel of mercy as he would be measuring ribbon in a milliner's store. Then there was the other two. 'Doc,' he called, 'your medicine is for the people we're on our way to help, not foolhardy fellows like these. If they want to put everyone's lives at risk then they can heal themselves.' Dan's voice was crusty, showing his unwillingness to give any leeway.

But 'Doc' was already rummaging in the black

medical bag from which she retrieved a jar of paste, bandage and scissors. She started across the cavern to where Tim Bradall's injuries were being inspected by Rory Blades. Jess Clarke moved to intercept her but Dan Hathaway got there first. He took the items out of her hand. 'The deputy can do the doctoring tonight,' he told her, his voice more gentle than it had been a moment ago. 'There's a shelf back there in the darkest part of the cave. Get yourself up there and get some sleep. You'll need plenty of energy tomorrow.'

Anne Hames knew by his manner that Dan Hathaway knew her true identity. She threw an angry look at Jess even though she had no idea of what she was accusing him. Still, she went into the darkness and the old man and the boy could hear her scrambling up the incline to the ledge which would be her bed for the night.

'You know who that is, don't you?' Jess said to Dan.

'Sure do.'

'How did you find out?'

'Jess, boy,' and Jess wasn't offended by the use of the word boy because nothing in Dan Hathaway's manner implied he was treating him as a child, 'when you've lived alone like I have you learn to recognize people by more than their face. You've got to know if people approaching are friend or foe so you watch the way they move. Their mannerisms. You understand?'

Jess nodded but it was clear he needed more of an explanation.

'I've lived around Wicker for more than ten years,' Dan explained, 'and in all that time I've never seen Doctor Billy Hames mount a horse as prettily as that girl done it back along the Dearborn.' He grinned. 'Didn't take much figuring who else had access to the doctor's bag.'

'Suppose not,' said Jess. 'Why didn't you say anything?'

'Same reason you didn't. Wouldn't have done any good. We couldn't send her back.' He paused for a moment then looked Jess square in the eyes. 'How did you find out it wasn't the doc?'

Jess felt himself flush as he recollected the feel of the girl in his hands. 'I didn't know until the horses became entangled.'

His reply wasn't really an answer to Dan's question and the stammered delivery made the old mountain man grin. 'But how did you know?'

There was a glint in Dan's eyes and Jess knew he was being teased. He grinned himself when he spoke. 'Let's just say that if we'd been on the mountain at the time she'd have pushed me clear off it.'

'That's what I figured when I came across the two of you,' chuckled Dan. 'She's sure got some spirit, that girl. Didn't have to come up here. Shows there's a whole lot of goodness in her.'

'It does,' said Jess who'd been thinking there were a lot of good things about her.

'But I'm not sure this is the wisest thing she'll ever do in her life.'

'That's my thought too,' said Jess.

'Well, you and me'll just have to take care of her and get her safely home.' With that he left Jess and took the salve and bandage to Rory Blades. 'Use that if you need

64

to, but don't trouble the doc. And if I were you, Deputy, I'd take all the weapons those two are carrying,' he indicated Tim and Reub, 'and stash them in your saddle-bags until we get back to Wicker. Nobody'll have any use for guns up in the Bitterroots.'

For the five hours they lay in the cave, sleep was unattainable to everyone. The fight had left behind an atmosphere of tension which prevented the mind from letting go of consciousness and the cold made the muscles of the body ache. As soon as Dan Hathaway rolled up the blanket he'd laid inside everyone else followed suit. Another small fire was lit and a pot of coffee brewed while the horses were saddled and packed as necessary.

More snow had fallen while they'd rested, extinguishing their tracks to the cave. Dan warned that progress would be slow but once they started up the mountain they'd be able to see Bridger Point, a distinguishing outcrop of rock near which Harv Prescott had lost his horse and killed the mountain lion. 'Keep in close formation,' he ordered. 'There are some stretches which can be scary on a clear day so I don't want anyone getting ahead of me.' He dictated the order he wanted them to maintain for the remainder of the journey, ensuring the brawlers were separated, although suspecting that the climb in deep snow would be enough of a challenge to banish any lingering hostile thought. So they began with Tim Bradall behind Dan, then 'Doc', Jess, Clay Brascoe and Reub. Rory Blades rode at the rear, charged with the task of keeping an eye open for signs of trouble from the riders ahead.

As Dan suspected, the trek took toll enough on energy and concentration so that other issues were forgotten. There was no sunlight, heavy cloud obliterated it and it was three hours before they realized that the day was now as light as it was going to be. Often they dismounted and walked with the horses, legs sinking knee deep whenever they missed the trail.

But Dan had been right about Bridger Point, even covered in snow like the rest of the mountain, it stood out clearly, guiding them as surely as the stars in the sky guided sailors at sea. No-one spoke, everyone conserving their strength for the toil of the climb.

They passed Bridger Point at midday, Dan choosing not to rest there knowing that a little way ahead the trail became more treacherous, and a rest before tackling that stretch would be more beneficial. He glanced at Anne Hames who was trudging determinedly at the head of her two horses, her hat still tied to her head with one scarf and the lower half of her face covered with another. She didn't look up at the landmark, simply kept her eyes on the tracks made by the horse in front. And behind her, Jess Clarke did likewise, except Dan suspected the young man's eyes were set a little higher than the ground and focused on the person ahead, not her animals.

A frozen hind leg stuck up out of the snow marking the location of Harv Prescott's dead horse. There was no sign of the dead mountain lion; it would remain concealed until the spring thaw. Here, Dan ordered a halt, figuring the horses had earned a ten minute breather for carrying them since passing Bridger Point, and because the track up the mountain narrowed considerably beyond this point. 'I'm gonna walk on ahead,' he told Rory Blades when everyone had dismounted. 'Need to check those stretches where the trail is little more than a ledge. The trouble with snow is that there ain't always under it what you think should be under it.' Using his rifle like a walking stick, stock down, he went off without another word.

In silence, most of the group watched as Dan prodded his way into the distance. Then Rory suggested loosening the cinches on the horses until they were ready to move on again.

'Where do you think he's going?' Clay Brascoe asked of no one in particular.

'Scouting ahead, I suppose,' said Tim Bradall who was nearest.

'Scouting! You think he's expecting to run into Indians up here?' Brascoe laughed. 'Say, Hadley, perhaps he's hoping to run into some Comanche with squaws for trade.'

Rory Blades snapped. 'That's enough, Brascoe.'

'Just having a little fun, Deputy. I reckon our mountain man is too old to remember what to do with a woman even if he came across a Comanche with a whole string of them.'

'That's enough,' repeated Rory.

''Course,' continued Clay Brascoe as though the deputy hadn't spoken, 'the women'd know what to do. Comanche teach them good. Teach them how to—'

'Shut up!' The almost frantic tone to Jess Clarke's youthful voice turned all heads in his direction.

Clay Brascoe pushed on his horse's rump so that he

67

could walk around it to stand six feet from Jess. He looked at the lad, a naive farm boy, his face red with embarrassment beneath a small cap with ear flaps.

'You carrying a gun beneath that coat, kid? If you are you'd better be prepared to use it 'cos nobody tells me when I can speak or what I can say.'

'Leave it, Brascoe,' said Rory Blades, 'and quit trying to stir up trouble.'

'Or what, Deputy. You gonna take my guns away and hide them in your saddle-bags?'

The deputy tried not to let his nervousness show. He had been entrusted with the task of rescuing the families stranded on the mountain and he knew he could do it if everyone was as anxious as him for a successful outcome. But Brascoe liked trouble, grinned at the misfortunes of others and was only too willing to encourage it in whatever way he could. Added to which was the feud between Hadley and Bradall which, even now as Brascoe tried to intimidate him, erupted behind him.

It was Reub Hadley who yelled, shouting an accusation at Tim Bradall. The horses between them had moved suddenly, one of them slipping or stumbling over something hidden under the snow and pushing against Hadley, dumping him on the ground. 'Spooked the horses,' he told anyone prepared to listen. 'Hoped they'd trample me. Tried to kill me like he did my sister.'

In Wicker it had been Tim Bradall's policy to ignore Reub Hadley's campaign of accusation against him. It hadn't been easy to bear the looks of scorn that had come from some men when he walked away without argument or fight, but Tim Bradall had no wish to confront his brother-in-law. Here, however, on the mountain, it wasn't possible to walk away, to find another refuge from Hadley's cruel words and the constant repetition had finally cracked his resolve, bringing about the brawl in the cave where they'd spent the night. Despite the salve he'd put on his neck, the collar of his coat still irritated the heat blisters and, despite the warnings issued by Dan and Rory, Hadley's words again agitated his anger. 'I didn't kill your sister,' he roared, 'and if I wanted to kill you it would be just as easy to push you over the edge.'

Reub, belligerent, back on his feet, ceased brushing the snow off himself. 'Been planning how to get rid of me?'

'No,'

'Just waiting for an opportunity when my back is turned.'

This attack on his character was the last straw. Tim Bradall moved menacingly forwards. A renewal of the previous night's fight only footsteps away, Rory Blades moved towards them shouting, orders to which neither man listened. Then, with a resounding crack, the ground below Reub's heels slid away leaving him balanced on the edge of the mountain. After that everything seemed to move in slow motion. Reub, sensing that a misstep would lead to his death, became momentarily paralyzed with indecision. The sound of the snow sliding away down the mountainside was almost like a clarion call, beckoning him to follow, and the sensation caused by the falling snow that swirled around his ankles was akin to a fast ebbing tide, dragging him backwards, unbalancing him, threatening with a force over which he had no control. He looked down at his feet as though trying to decide which one it would be safest to move first. Undecided, he looked behind him at the white emptiness, at the billowing snow hitting outcrops a hundred feet below. Then he slipped, his feet going into the space behind, his knees hitting the edge of the mountain trail, then his body slipping over until only his head and arms were in sight. Desperately he grabbed at the ledge and hung there, his gloved hands seeking an unlikely hold.

Tim Bradall's reaction was instantaneous, diving forward, arms outstretched, both hands grabbing for his brother-in-law's wrists. He caught them, gripped them tightly and peered over the edge into the upturned face of his tormentor. Eyes wide and colour drained it was a picture of fear and desperation. Reub dangled, his legs scrabbling at the mountainside for some place which would give him a foothold and hope, but the snow-covered rock gave no such refuge. Despite Tim's grip on his wrist, gravity was winning the tug of war.

Catching hold of any part of Reub had been Tim Bradall's first goal and he had been successful, but now he realized he hadn't the strength to haul the man back up to the trail. Indeed, as he lay on his stomach, he could feel himself sliding ever closer to the edge. He, too, would perish if he continued to hold on to Reub in this manner. 'Reub,' he said, his features so contorted with effort that he seemed to snarl, 'I didn't kill your sister,' and with these words he let go with his left hand. Reub yelled and grasped at the air with his released right hand as though reaching for an invisible bar to hold.

70

Relinquishing his hold on Reub's right hand had been a last ditch effort on Tim Bradall's part, his intention being to reach down and grab the collar of Reub's coat, which would not only give him a more secure hold but also the ability to gain some leverage to pull Reub back onto firm ground. Reub, throwing up his hand, would have undone Tim's plan and most likely would have caused them both to plunge to their doom if assistance in three forms hadn't arrived at that moment.

When Reub Hadley first slipped over the edge of the mountain, Tim Bradall wasn't alone in reacting. Young Jess Clarke, still standing beside his horse, snatched a rope from the saddle and, when Reub's hand went clear of the ground, he threw it with the same accuracy he'd attained on the ranch roping a calf's hind legs. And, in similar fashion, he looped the rope twice around the saddle horn to hold the captured target in place. However, any satisfaction with his marksmanship was tempered by the sight of Anne Hames running towards the edge of the mountain.

At first, Anne Hames grabbed Tim Bradall's ankles, trying in vain to pull him backwards to safer ground but, try as she would, their combined weight was too much for her to budge. Catching sight of the rope that secured Reub's right hand, she gave her attention to that, and, much to Jess Clarke's despair, she moved closer to the edge. For a moment, as she looked down at Reub Hadley, she seemed to totter, as though affected by the enormity of the fall that lay before her. Then she grabbed the rope and began to haul on it until Reub's hand and arm were clear of the edge.

Rory Blades, too, had joined in the effort to save Reub Hadley. By the time the rope Jess had thrown had tightened around Reub's right arm, he had flung himself forward, lying half on Tim Bradall and reaching down to grip Reub Hadley's left sleeve as though attempting to save both men with his action. Between them they began to make progress, shuffling backwards, inching Reub's head into view, then his shoulders.

Jess urged the horse two slow steps backward which was sufficient pull for Reub to clamber his right leg over the top. Less than a minute later he was lying on his back, breathing deeply, his ordeal over. Rory Blades and Tim Bradall sat in the snow, heads bowed as they recovered from their exertion. No one spoke.

Anne Hames, too, sat in the snow, picking up handfuls and letting it sift through her gloved fingers as though in idle contemplation. Even though he expected her to show nothing but anger at his attention, Jess was unable to hide his concern for her any longer. Standing in front of her he waited until she looked up. The brown eyes didn't look at him with scorn. Instead they were red and wet with tears. The silence of the post-drama moments had allowed the knowledge of her action, the closeness of death, to seep through her defences. It had drained her physically and emotionally and she didn't know if the sickly feeling in her stomach was due to overexertion, tiredness or fear. She didn't even care, at that moment, that Jess Clarke knew she was crying.

Jess sat down beside her. He didn't speak because he didn't know what to say. He wanted to tell her how brave she'd been but figured words might force a reply from her and conversation could break what existed between them at this moment. They sat shoulder to shoulder and Jess believed that Anne was leaning against him, accepting his support. He was happy to have it that way as long as she wanted it.

Presently, Anne stood and made her way towards the horses. She'd only taken a couple of steps when she stumbled. Her booted feet slipped and, awkwardly, she went full-length into the snow. Such was her attempt to save herself that she twisted as she fell and flung up her arms to prevent landing heavily on her shoulder. Her hands, however, caught against the brim of her hat and dislodged it. As she lay in the snow her long, light brown hair, spread around her head like a ragged-edged halo.

For a moment no one spoke as realization dawned on the group.

'Well,' said Clay Brascoe, who had played no part in the earlier event, 'what have we here?' He walked across to where Anne lay, looking down at her, grinning at thoughts which didn't need voicing, then turning his attention to Jess Clarke who was now on his feet. 'Been keeping this to yourself, kid? Knew there was something wrong about the way you never took your eyes off the doc. Suppose you and her were hot as Hades last night while the rest of us were freezing in that cave.'

'Don't you talk about Anne like that.'

'You telling me what to say again, kid? I ain't forgotten we still have a reckoning between us.' He reached down and grabbed Anne's arm, half pulling her to her feet. 'So,' he continued, 'do you want to settle it before or after I've finished with her?'

He pulled again at Anne's arm but stopped suddenly when he felt cold metal pressed against his ear. 'You let go of that girl,' rasped the voice of Dan Hathaway, 'and make sure you don't touch her again otherwise I'll blast your head clean off your shoulders. And don't make the mistake of thinking that I won't follow through with my threat. I've killed men before that needed killing and it's never bothered me too much after. In your case, I'll forget your name the moment I kick your carcass off the mountain.'

CHAPTER THREE

The next section of the trail was the most difficult to negotiate, it being steep and narrow, but with Dan leading the way and everyone else placing their feet where his had been they reached a gentler incline without mishap. Even here, though, the snow was deep and walking in it sapped everyone's energy and required their total concentration. This accounted for the lack of conversation as they made their way on the mountain but the image of Dan Hathaway's rifle pressed against Clay Brascoe's right ear was still clear in everyone's mind.

During those moments, the colour had drained from Brascoe's face but, as soon as the old man uncocked his Winchester, Brascoe regained his aggressive attitude. He threw looks at Anne and Jess that carried warnings to both. He didn't consider the business between them to be at an end – when the opportunity arose he would have satisfaction from both.

Dan Hathaway had seen and understood the unspoken message that had passed from Clay Brascoe to the young people and his thumb returned to the hammer of his rifle. A man who needs killing, he'd thought, but there were two reasons for not doing it now. First, they were a small enough rescue party, every man would be necessary when they reached the stranded travellers. The second reason was Rory Blades. In the past, Dan had killed two men without allowing them the opportunity to defend themselves. One had been a fellow mountain man who had tried to turn a tribe of Flathead Indians against him so that he could get Dan's pelts and traps. He'd caught him skinning beaver by the river and had shot him dead with the butchered animal still in his hands. The second man had stolen Dan's horse, left him afoot in the high grass land, not caring if he lived or died. Knowing his horse was too tired to travel far, Dan had trailed the man. He came across him at nightfall, drinking coffee he'd brewed on a small fire. His surprise at Dan's appearance was only surpassed by his surprise when a bullet from Dan's six-gun hit him between the eyes. Dan finished the coffee and slept the night across the fire from the body of the man he'd killed. Dan had no regrets about the killings. They were two men who deserved to die, who would have done to others what they'd done to him. He'd left them to rot where they lay, probably undiscovered until their bones turned to dust and were spread across the land by the wind. He rarely thought of them, didn't even know the name of the horse thief. He never spoke of them and no-one knew he had done the deeds. There were no witnesses.

But if he killed Clay Brascoe now, Deputy Sheriff Rory Blades would call it murder and would want to put him in jail when they got back to Wicker. Being locked up wasn't a situation that sat too well on Dan's spirit. So he relaxed his grip on his rifle. 'Keep a close eye on Brascoe,' he told Rory Blades. 'I don't expect he'll cause anymore mischief while we're climbing but he's not a man I'd like to show my back too.'

Rory told Dan the story of the rescue of Reub Hadley. 'Brascoe did nothing to help,' he explained. 'If that's the way he intends to behave I don't know why he's come along.'

Dan was beginning to wonder the same thing because so far the gun-hand had only shown interest in antagonizing other members of the group. He let his gaze wander over the other four people. Tim Bradall and Reub Hadley sat together, not speaking, but their silence seemed more companionable, as though the recent bitterness had abated. Anne Hames and Jess Clarke stood near the horses, Anne rubbing her arm where Clay Brascoe had held her and Jess recoiling the lasso he had used to save Reub. Anne was talking, praising his ability with the rope. Jess smiled, not wanting to add anything lest he seemed boastful but pleased that she saw something in him to admire.

'Let's get going,' Dan said and set about tightening the saddle girth of his horse.

Reub Hadley spoke to his brother-in-law. 'Why did you say you that?' he asked. 'About not killing Caroline,' he added.

'Because it's true.'

Reub nodded, slowly, accepting Tim Bradall's words. 'But why then? Why say it when I was hanging on to you for my life?'

'Because I couldn't hold you any longer. I was going to

have to let you go. I needed to tell you again that I hadn't killed her so that you would know it was the truth.' He stood and began to walk towards the horses.

Reub followed. 'Where is she, Tim? Where is Caroline?'

'I don't know. She left me, Reub. That's all I can tell you.'

'You mean it's all you will tell me. You know more. I'm sure you do.'

'Go back home, Reub. Following me won't lead you to her.'

Less than an hour later they came across the stranded travellers. Deep snow and broken trees marked the path of the avalanche and beyond they could see the little gathering of wagons and makeshift canvas shelters that had been assembled to provide some little protection from the weather. Although there had been no snow that day, the wind had blown a thin covering over the tents but an effort had been made to keep the ground around the camp clear of deep drifts. A fire burned crisply in front of the tents, smoke climbing high one moment then spreading with the wind the next. Unaware of the approaching riders and huddled so close together that they looked like a dark chimney sticking up out of the snow, four men conversed in a circle.

Reub Hadley drew his rifle from its scabbard. 'I'll let them know we're here,' he declared and pointed the gun skywards.

'Don't pull that trigger,' snapped Dan Hathaway. 'Gunshots are well able to start avalanches. They'll see us soon enough.'

In fact it was a child who spotted them. Little Lucy Fetterman, weary and cold from another day on the mountain, had left the cramped enclosure where her brothers argued and her mother sewed, in search of her father. She found him talking with Mr Brewster, Mr Bent and Mr Houseman near the point where the freight wagon had been swept away by the snow. Her mother had told her she must never go there but her father was there so it would be safe for her to do so now. Then something moved in the whiteness beyond her father. Then another movement. Then a shape. 'Pa,' she shouted, and when he looked her way she pointed down the mountain, beyond the route of the avalanche. 'Glory be,' she heard Cal Brewster say and the four men spread apart. Her pa called, 'Go and tell your ma, Lucy,' then began walking with the others towards the new arrivals.

Being a Wicker man, Cal knew some of the people in the party. He exchanged greetings with Dan Hathaway and Rory Blades, nodded recognition to Jess and Tim Bradall, looked with undisguised surprise at Anne Hames and undisguised suspicion at Clay Brascoe. Finally, he said, 'Howdy,' when introduced to the stranger, Reub Hadley, before introducing Sam Fetterman, Roy Houseman and Charlie Bent. Charlie Bent was the driver of the coach bringing the saloon girls from Butte.

'We expected you two days ago,' Cal began. 'We were thinking Harv hadn't got through, thought perhaps we should be making plans to get out of here. There's no way of fixing one of the wagons but I don't suppose they'd get through the deep snow even if they were prime. Besides, we'd need to clear away all the debris the avalanche brought with it before we could roll another yard.' He pointed at the avalanche trail. 'Tried to clear away some of the timber. Gave us something to do when it wasn't snowing and kept the horses active. Poor beasts are suffering in this cold worse than we are.'

Dan Hathaway voiced the opinion that had grown more firm with him the higher they had climbed. 'You're right about the wagons. They'll have to stay here until spring. All we can do is get the people down from the mountain. We've brought six spare horses.'

'Yeah,' said Roy Houseman, 'that's enough. There are twenty-one people here and now we have twenty-two horses.'

'Understand some of your people are injured,' said Dan.

'Nathan Creek died,' said Cal. 'Horse fell on him and broke some ribs. Bust something inside him. Nothing we could do to help. Doubt if a doctor could have helped him but he might have had some morphine to take away his pain.'

'Anyone else need treatment?' asked Anne Hames. 'My father wasn't in town when news of your predicament reached us, but I came along to do whatever I could.'

' 'Preciate that, Miss. Roy's boy broke an arm but I pushed the bone back in place and tied it with a splint. You can take a look if you like. Did things like that when I was in the army. Had to when out on patrol and no medical officer within four days' ride.'

'My wife,' said Sam Fetterman, 'she was thrown from the wagon and hit her head on a wheel. She was unconscious for a long time. She tells me she's OK now but I ain't sure she's telling the truth. If you'd talk to her I'd be obliged.'

By this time, the womenfolk and youngsters of the families had begun to gather and, although they were all wrapped in many layers of clothing to combat the low temperature, there was a sense of excitement akin to that on a Fourth of July morning. Pale as their faces were, there was no hiding their sense of relief that the township of Wicker had sent out a party to guide them off the mountain. One woman carried a coffee pot and a collection of tin mugs to welcome the rescuers and, because no snow had fallen that day, the women had grabbed the opportunity to bake so there were biscuits to pass around.

Jack Houseman, the boy with the broken arm, was sixteen. Satisfied that he wasn't suffering excessive pain, Anne Hames did no more than give Cal Brewster's tight splint a cursory inspection and told Jack that he must see her father as soon as he got to Wicker. One or two other children had minor injuries but pioneer mothers had ample treatments for those. Sarah Fetterman, however, was a different matter. She was a slim woman and her face, already pale with the cold, had adopted a gaunt expression by means of half moons of darkness beneath her eyes. The orbs of the eyes themselves were opaque and seemed to have sunk back into her head. Her lips were blue and although she tried to stretch them in a smile of welcome she fooled no one. Even Jess Clarke, who had little experience of injury and sickness, knew instinctively that she was in pain.

There was a lump the size of an egg to the left of the crown of Sarah Fetterman's head, and a jagged, three-inch line of dried blood where the scalp had split. Anne examined it as gently as possible but Sarah moaned and flinched repeatedly. Anne knew that the injury was beyond her knowledge but thought it possible that the skull was fractured. Recalling how her father had tended a cowboy who'd been pistol-whipped by Sheriff Grayson for firing off his gun on Main Street, she applied a damp cloth to the swollen area and tied it tightly in place with a length of bandage.

The closed coach which was bringing Duke Ferris's saloon girls from Butte was thirty yards from the other four vehicles. This gap had developed shortly before the snow slid down the mountain, when Charlie Bent had slowed his team on the slippery terrain. He'd been unable to do anything for those ahead when the avalanche occurred. Helplessly, he'd watched the moments of mayhem and the resulting melee. Afterwards, when it was clear they were destined to remain on the mountain for a few days, no one told the girls they had to stay where they were, but nor did anyone suggest they should move closer. Nor did anyone send a message to let them know that the party from Wicker had arrived. It was Cherokee Lil who became aware of the activity further along the trail and, seeing the newcomers, broke the news to the others. Wrapped in long coats and blankets that Cal had handed out from

Lars Freidrikson's freight wagon, they scurried through the snow.

By this time, Anne Hames had gone back to the Fetterman enclosure to examine Sarah's head wound and the men were dismounted, drinking coffee and confirming with each other that there was no hope of getting the wagons down the mountain. All they could do was secure them where they stood, lash them to trees or rocks, and hope that they weren't swept off the mountain by strong wind or snow slides. 'There won't be much these people'll be able to take with them,' Dan declared. 'Carrying us will be enough for the horses to cope with. Perhaps an extra bag of clothes or valuables. Nothing more.'

Clay Brascoe took two huge gulps from the tin mug and let the coffee burn its way down to his stomach. He had no interest in the plans that were being made to get the people off the mountain nor in the reasons for leaving the wagons behind. He hadn't come up here to dig snow or haul wagons or even to guide people down to the township below. If people got themselves stuck on a mountain in winter that was their problem. He was here for only one reason and the swaddled figures approaching carefully across the snow covered ground between him and the remote coach brought to his eyes a glint of satisfaction that was only generated by the prospect of personal gain.

Cherokee Lil reached him first. Recognition almost stopped her in her tracks. 'You,' she said. She didn't like Clay Brascoe. She had little reason to like him. He was cruel to her in every way it was possible to be cruel. But she knew he got his pleasure from cruelty. He was cruel to nearly all the girls. 'Duke sent you to help us?' Her tone carried the implication of disbelief, that he, of all the people employed by Duke Ferris, should have been sent to rescue them.

'Duke sent me,' he said, not looking at her, but staring over her head in the direction from which she had come.

The following four girls, Ruby, arm-in-arm with Talahassee, and Conchita, the Mexican girl, scurrying to keep up with the long striding Trixie, passed Brascoe without a word, though, from the looks they cast in his direction, they knew and feared him. But the reaction of the sixth girl was completely different, recognizing him and calling his name when she was still ten yards away.

'Clay,' she shouted, trying to break into a run but cautiously, fear of slipping in the snow restricting her movement to an ungainly, hurried walk. When she reached him she flung her arms around his neck in wanton fashion, clinging to him. 'You came for me, Clay.' Until he'd left Butte, Cimmaron Kate had attached herself to Clay Brascoe whenever he'd entered the Prairie Queen where she'd worked. His reputation had been insurance for her, the perception that she was Clay Brascoe's girl saved her from violence from anyone else's hand. It was an insurance she was unwilling to yield and when news arrived that Duke wanted girls to work in his new Wicker saloon, Cimmaron Kate was among the first to volunteer.

'Cimmaron!' Brascoe had no more feeling for this girl than he did any other but, for a while, her servile attention to him had amused him. However, by the time he'd quit Butte that amusement had been long exhausted. Still, to be singled out here, on a bleak mountain, by the most attractive girl in the bunch, to his mind made him the envy of his companions. 'Sure. Came all the way up here just to rescue you,' he lied, the thought that stringing her along could provide some mischief, dancing in his mind.

The trouble he hoped for was closer at hand than he expected. Cimmaron's arms were sliding down his neck, her gloved hands coming to rest against his chest. Her head was turned away from him, looking across the low flames of the camp-fire where the other riders from Wicker stood. For a moment her look was one of surprise, disbelief, then she laughed. It was a short laugh. One which was filled with scorn. 'Well, well,' she said. 'What are you doing here? No stray cattle to round up on this mountain.'

Brascoe looked across the fire. Tim Bradall watched them, transfixed, as though his boots had frozen to the hillside, unable to move even if he wanted to.

Survival for men like Clay Brascoe depended upon cunning, speed and an ability to assess situations quickly. That being so, it required only one look at each of the faces of Tim Bradall and the girl he knew as Cimmaron Kate to know he had the power to use one to goad the other. He'd forced several pathetic creatures like Tim Bradall to reach for a gun in the past and now they were nothing but a knife mark on his gun butt. Unhesitatingly he pulled Cimmaron to him and kissed her fiercely, the sort of kiss a whiskey filled trail hand gives a saloon girl before his money is all spent. He held their faces together a long time. When they parted he muttered, 'Same old Cimmaron,' then thrust her aside signalling he was done with her for now, that he had more important matters to attend to. But he didn't move. He looked across the fire, a slim, sly smile on his lips as his eyes met those of Tim Bradall.

Tim Bradall half turned away but the voice of Cimmaron Kate checked him. 'If you've come looking to take me back to that dirt farm in Arizona then you've had a wasted journey. Nothing you offer can tempt me away from Clay.' She grabbed at Brascoe's sleeve, a proprietorial gesture, spots of spittle clinging to her lips, her jaw jutting forward in antagonism.

'I haven't,' he replied. 'I didn't know you were here.' Tim turned away, aware that the exchange had stopped all other conversation.

Clay Brascoe, determined to encourage the tension, spoke again. 'You mean Cimmaron here is your wife? The one you're accused of killing?'

'Killing?' Cimmaron's short laugh once more was full of scorn. 'He couldn't kill me. Couldn't do anything but nurse his precious cattle.'

'The stock was our livelihood. Our wealth.'

'Wealth,' she retorted. 'I didn't see any wealth. Just work, work, work. Sunup to sundown. No one to talk to for days and days. No one to visit for miles and miles.' She paused. The frowns across her brow smoothed away. An unkind smile touched her lips, her head dipped to one side so that she could see his face more clearly through the smoke. 'Of course, I sometimes had visitors. A whole troop of boys in blue to entertain while you were out on the range. They were the best days. Didn't know about those, did you?'

'Caroline!' The voice was strong, angry, austere.

Cimmaron hadn't taken much notice of the other men on her husband's side of the fire but she looked now at the face to his left. It was a slim face, one she hadn't seen for twelve years but which she instantly recognized. 'Reuben!'

'Yeah,' Clay Brascoe grinned. 'Your brother. He's been fighting with your husband ever since we left Wicker.'

Her hands fluttered before her face, defensively, as though making a belated attempt to hide her identity. The gesture, however was only momentary. With an arrogant lift of her head she faced her brother. 'It's true,' she said. 'I'm not going back to a life of dust and drought in summer and freezing cold in winter. Fearful of Indians and fevers and mind-numbing loneliness. I'm finished with it. I want people around me and nice clothes.'

Reub Hadley observed her without speaking then looked at Tim Bradall who had walked away from the fire. He followed him. 'Did you know what she was doing?'

'When she left me she went to work in a hotel in Flagstaff. She's right about it being a hard life out on the plains, but we knew that before we bought the land. She wanted a homestead as much as I did but I guess she expected more out of life than what she got with me. One day everything was just different. She was empty of happiness and there was nothing I could do.' He paused, trying to find some more words to say. 'After she went some neighbours told me about the type of work she was doing in Flagstaff. I knew then I didn't want her back. Farming is my life. It may seem like scratching a living to some people but it's what I know best. But I chose to move on. I heard that the land here in Montana was good for raising cattle herds so I sold the strip in Arizona and came north. Last I heard of Caroline was that she'd taken up with a gambler. Supposed to be heading for San Francisco. I didn't know she was in Butte or anywhere in this vicinity. I'm not looking for her, Reub. I don't want her back.'

Reub Hadley rubbed his jaw. The anger of recent days rose again, filling his chest and his head like air in a fully stretched balloon. But he couldn't vent it at Tim Bradall who, only a few hours earlier, had risked his own life to save him from plunging over the precipice. His eyes sought out his sister. He was shocked by her appearance and brazen attitude, found it difficult to accept the evidence before him of the woman she'd become. He watched her walk away with Clay Brascoe, could see her talking to him, anxious to have him respond. Clay Brascoe, however, was walking with purposeful stride, apparently uninterested in Caroline, but suddenly he threw a look over his left shoulder, back to where Reub and Tim stood, and again that sly grin touched his face. He put an arm around Caroline's shoulders, pulled her to him, possessively, and laughed. Caroline smiled up at him believing, at first, that it was her and her alone who captivated him. Then she, too, looked back across the fire and saw her brother watching them. The smile died on her face. When Brascoe walked on towards the place where she and the other girls had camped, she slowly followed.

'I'm concerned for Mrs Fetterman,' Anne Hames reported to Dan Hathaway and Rory Blades. 'My father needs to see her as soon as possible.'

'If the snow holds off we ought to have her back in Wicker tomorrow night,' said Rory Blades.

'Mrs Fetterman has double vision. I'm worried that she has a fractured skull,' explained Anne. 'Walking and horse riding won't improve her situation.'

'Not much we can do about that. She can't stay here,' said Rory.

'I know,' said Anne. 'That's why I'm concerned.'

'Perhaps another night's rest will help,' said Dan.

'I was thinking I'd like to start back with her immediately,' said Anne. 'If we can get down to the cave at Two Horse Pass by nightfall we can make an early start from there in the morning.'

'The horses worked hard getting us up here,' said Rory. 'It won't be any easier for them going down.'

'That's true,' said Dan Hathaway, 'but at least it'll be warmer for them in the cave overnight than being exposed on the mountain. Those beasts that have come from Butte will be pleased to be active again.'

'Do you think we can make it down to the cave by nightfall?' Rory asked Dan.

'There's been no snow to cover our tracks. That should make it easier. If we can avoid arguments among ourselves that'll help, too. And I dare say these people are eager to reach the hospitality that Wicker has to offer.'

So, decision made, they set about organizing the evacuation of the camp. The men secured the wagons, dismantled the shelters and lashed down the contents in the hope of recovering everything when the snows had gone. The women packed small bags of clothing and treasured items that they chose to take with them. Those horses that had been used to pull the wagons from Butte weren't equipped with proper riding harness so the saddles were strapped to the backs of those animals which would carry the women and youngsters whilst the men folk would manage as best they were able with adapted dray harnesses.

Preparations were almost complete when Jess Clarke came across Anne Hames as she checked the medical bag before attaching it to the saddle of her horse. 'Ready to go?' he asked.

Without turning to face him she nodded her head.

'You OK, Anne?'

Again she nodded but with little enthusiasm. Jess walked around the other side of her horse so that he could see her across its back. Swaddled in her clothes again, prepared for the journey ahead, there was little to see of her face. Her brown eyes looked up at him, held his for a moment then looked down at the straps she was tying around the handles of the black bag.

'What is it?' he inquired.

'I shouldn't be here,' she said. 'I'm a fraud.' Jess said nothing, waited for an explanation. 'The minor injuries were taken care of by the families themselves and Mr Brewster fixed the broken arm.'

'That doesn't make you a fraud. Those same things

would have been done if your father had been able to ride with us. You said you came to do what you could. The fact that there was nothing for you to do when you got here doesn't detract from your intention.'

Anne rested her head against the saddle, her words spoken into the leather so that Jess had to struggle to hear her. 'I'm not sure I could have fixed the broken arm,' she said, 'and the one person who does need a doctor I can't do anything for.' She raised her eyes to him again. 'So what was the point of coming? What was I thinking? That because I'm my father's daughter I know as much as him? I'm a fraud, Jess.'

Although he considered her self-criticism misplaced, he recognized her desire to help and heal as genuine needs in her personality. That was why he liked being near her. 'Listen,' he said, 'you're no more of a fraud than I am. I came because I thought I was strong enough to help clear away the rubble from the avalanche so that the wagons could continue down to Wicker. Now we're here we know that such a plan is unworkable. If we'd known that before we left Wicker it would have been sufficient to send Mr Hathaway with six spare horses. He found the way here and he'll guide the way back.' He smiled at her hoping for the same in return because as entranced as he was by her dark eyes when her mood was serious, with a smile in them they warmed him better than the morning sun.

'Mrs Fetterman,' she said. 'She needs to be examined by a proper doctor. I don't think it's right to move her until she is.'

'But that's not possible. You're not responsible for the

situation, Anne, and you being here doesn't make matters worse. The way I see it,' Jess told her, 'there isn't any choice. We must travel, so the sooner we get underway the better it'll be. There may be some risk to moving Mrs Fetterman but there's a risk to everyone if we stay here. There's a lot of snow on the mountain and another avalanche is always possible.'

Anne knew he was right, knew also that she was justified in being concerned for the well-being of Mrs Fetterman but suspected that her irksome attitude owed more to pride than she cared to admit. She had hoped to return to Wicker with her name on every survivor's lips, with her healing prowess the subject of numerous tales so that the townspeople wouldn't forget her. 'What use have I been,' she asked, 'coming up here as if I could do what my father does and finding that I'm no value at all.'

'How can you say that? You saved a man's life earlier today.' The look in her eyes told him she was about to deny his words but he spoke again, emphasizing the claim. 'It was your quickness that saved him, Anne. That rope could easily have slipped off his hand if you hadn't grabbed it. Then to get so near the edge to haul up Mr Hadley took a lot of nerve.'

'You were the one who acted quickly,' she said, embarrassed slightly that he was giving her so much credit. 'Throwing that rope with such accuracy was what saved him. That and Mr Bradall clinging to him.'

Jess recalled the scene and knew that at that point Tim Bradall was close to letting go of his brother-in-law. That was why Reub Hadley's hand was in the air for him to

92

rope, that was why Anne and Rory Blades' intervention had been paramount. 'Reckon it needed all of us to save him,' he said.

'Reckon it did,' she said, impishly copying his phrase, finally allowing his words to placate her sense of failure. Jess didn't object to her teasing, despite her face being partially covered by a scarf, he could tell by her eyes that she was smiling. 'Well,' she added more soberly, 'all except that awful Clay Brascoe. It's because of me that he's trying to pick a fight with you, isn't it?'

'Don't worry about that.' Jess's voice held more confidence than he felt.

Just at that moment the object of their discussion strode towards them. Clay Brascoe carried an old, leather satchel in his right hand and a small, grubby, linen bag in the other. Charlie Bent scurried at his side, asking questions to which Brascoe gave no answers. The other men, chores completed, were assembling to supervise the allocation of mounts to the families.

'What's the trouble?' Rory Blades asked Charlie.

'This fella took those bags from my coach. I wanna know what's in 'em. Hidden away they wuz. Nobody told me they were there. This fella just lifts the floor of the coach, pulls 'em out and walks away with 'em. Wut's in 'em, thet's wut I wanna know.'

Those gathered looked to Clay Brascoe for an explanation but none was forthcoming. He turned his back and began tying the bags to his saddle.

'Well, Brascoe. What's all this about?' Rory asked.

Brascoe continued his task, spoke without turning. 'None of your business, Deputy.'

'Everything connected with this expedition is my business.'

'This ain't,' said Brascoe, 'so quit pushing.'

'Mister,' the quiet voice of Dan Hathaway seemed edged with weariness, 'every expedition has a leader and when that leader wants information it's given to him. Now you knew when you came along that Deputy Blades was in charge and nothing's altered since we left Wicker. You answer his question or we'll take a look in those bags for ourselves.'

Clay Brascoe turned his head so that he could see the old man over his left shoulder. He also saw the Winchester cradled in Dan's arms and pointed in his direction. 'Old man,' he said, 'I'm getting mighty sick of you holding a gun on me.'

'If you want to do something about it then make your move.'

Clay Brascoe stood perfectly still; seconds passed as though he was contemplating his chances of unbuttoning his coat, drawing his Colt, turning and firing before the old mountain man pulled the trigger on his rifle. 'Money,' he said eventually. 'There's money in the bags. It belongs to Duke Ferris.'

'Looks like a lot,' observed Rory Blades.

'Sold his place in Butte. This is the proceeds. Had it put in the bottom of the coach so that no one would see it being shipped across to Wicker. Didn't want anyone getting any ideas about it. Didn't want anyone getting sticky fingers.' His last sentence was directed at Charlie Bent.

'Hey,' said Charlie, 'I've worked for Duke a long time.

He can trust me.'

'Oh yeah,' said Brascoe in a manner that cast doubt on Charlie's honesty.

'Cudda told me it wuz there,' grumbled Charlie Bent.

'And this is why you came along,' stated Dan Hathaway. 'In case the coach was abandoned. You wanted to make sure the money was safe.'

'Well you didn't think I came to rescue a bunch of whores, did you?' Brascoe derived satisfaction from Reub Hadley's reaction to his use of the word *whores*, and ignored Dan's comment that until now no one had had any idea why he'd come along. 'A man can always buy another whore,' he said, looking at Reub, grinning, taunting him.

Reub flung himself forward, his right arm hooking in a swing at Brascoe's head. Tim Bradall tried to wrestle him away but only after Reub's fist had glanced across Brascoe's cheek.

'That's enough,' yelled Rory Blades, and Dan, holding his rifle across his chest, stepped between Reub and Clay Brascoe to put an end to the fight.

'The next time you come at me you'd better have a gun in your hand,' Brascoe snapped at Reub Hadley, but Dan sensed the anger in the words was nothing more than disguise. Secretly, he suspected, Clay Brascoe enjoyed Reub's attack and the possibility of provoking a gunfight at some future point.

'You're some piece of work, Brascoe,' declared Dan.

'Yeah, you've got the upper hand at the moment, old man, but it won't always be that way. My chance'll come and you'll be dead before you've even latched on to the

95

fact. You know something, old man, only one of us is coming off this mountain alive.'

Rory Blades declared there was work to do. If they wanted to get down to Two Falls Pass by nightfall they needed to get underway. The group split up to undertake their own preparations. While the families and saloon girls were summoned, and horses were packed and saddled, Dan spoke to Jess. 'That critter Brascoe is going to be behind me all the way to the foot of the mountain. I'd appreciate you being my eyes on the journey. Keep an eye on him if you can.' After Jess agreed he spoke again. 'I don't like the way he looks at you and the girl. He has evil intentions, Jess. If the time comes that you have to kill him then don't hesitate. Just do it. Some men need killing.'

They travelled in Indian file, twenty-eight people in assorted coverings of coats, cloaks and blankets to ward off the cold, Dan Hathaway at the front, guiding his horse to step in the tracks that had been made on the way up earlier that day. The Houseman family followed Dan, five of them in total, the youngest, a boy of three, riding with his pa. Then Rory Blades came ahead of the widow, Mary Creek, and her two sons, with Tim Bradall and Reub Hadley separating them from the five members of the Fetterman family. Anne Hames stayed as close to the Fettermans as possible, trying to watch Sarah Fetterman, determined to be at her side if the journey became an ordeal for the injured woman. Jess Clarke rode behind Anne then Charlie Bent led the six saloon girls. Cimmaron Kate was the last of the girls and behind her rode Clay Brascoe. Finally, came Cal Brewster with the spare horse.

For Dan Hathaway, the descent was straightforward. Even in the dull light the imprints were deep enough to be clearly seen so the trail ahead held no surprises. Even so, the pace he set was unhurried, not wanting to over-burden those animals that had made the climb that morning. However, several of the travellers were not experienced riders and some of those that were, rode without the benefit of saddle and stirrups. None had ridden in such dire conditions before. Consequently, by the time they'd negotiated the narrowest stretch of the trail, they were strung out over a distance of about half a mile. The biggest gap would have developed in front of the Fetterman family if Tim Bradall and Reub Hadley had not chosen to keep in sight of those behind rather than those in front. The Creek family and the others in front were soon lost from the sight of Tim and Reub. Although Mr Fetterman had maintained a cautious pace in consideration of his wife, her injury wasn't the major reason for travelling slower than those in front. It soon became clear that the horse the youngest daughter rode was in difficulties. Frequently it stopped, reluctant to move on, shivering one moment, blowing with cough-like spasms the next. When they reached the point where the frozen leg of Harv Prescott's horse pointed to the sky, the decision was made that the beast should suffer no longer. They halted there, waited for the arrival of Charlie Bent and the girls, Clay Brascoe and Cal Brewster with the spare horse.

Seeing the Fettermans stop and dismount, Tim

Bradall and Reub Hadley turned around and rode back to join them. Anne Hames took the opportunity to speak with Mrs Fetterman who, she was relieved to see, was coping well with the journey. She reported the same to Jess who was pleased that she now seemed to gravitate naturally to where he was when they had time to kill. He estimated the time waiting for the arrival of the spare horse and swapping saddle and packs would be fifteen minutes. When Charlie Bent arrived he was persuaded by Tim Bradall to continue on the trail to catch up with the rest of the party and let them know the cause of the delay. They would join them at the cave at Two Falls Pass.

Cal Brewster looked the horse over and declared it was dying on its feet. 'The cold has done for it,' he said. 'Pneumony I shouldn't wonder.' Everyone dismounted while the changeover took place. 'Walk my horse on aways with you,' he told Jess when it was completed. 'I'll put a bullet in this one when you're clear. Doesn't pay to let the others see one of their own being killed. Some horses spook easily.'

In keeping with the rest of the expedition, Clay Brascoe had done nothing to help the Fetterman family. His mind, however, had been very busy. With the old man and his rifle further down the mountain he now had the opportunity to amuse himself. His thoughts lingered first on Anne Hames. He pictured her, tearful and crying for mercy and smiled at the knowledge that her pleading was part of his pleasure. Then he shifted his thoughts to the kid who was always at her side. Twice he'd confronted him, told him what he could or couldn't say, and that was twice too often. The old man had befriended him, too, which was another reason to put a bullet in him. Perhaps now was the time.

Finally, however, his attention had settled on Reub Hadley. Too headstrong to be any good as a gunfighter, he guessed, too much ruled by his temper and too easily provoked. When Cal Brewster announced it was time to go, Clay got to his feet and began opening his coat, letting his right hand brush against the butt of his pistol, happy with the sensation. 'Come on Cimmaron,' he called, 'if you're as tardy when you're working in the Red Garter you'll not only end up the poorest whore west of the Missouri but also out on the street without a roof over your head.'

Cimmaron Kate, who was already on her way to the horses, tried to laugh off his comments but her brother reacted exactly as Brascoe had hoped.

'Don't you speak to my sister like that,' said Reub.

'Hey, just giving good advice. Duke Ferris is running the only brothel in Wicker and he carries no passengers. If Cimmaron wants to work in that town she'll have to be busy all the time or there'll be no place for her at The Red Garter. What then? She'll be giving herself away to the blacksmith so she can sleep in the shed where he shoes the horses.'

With a roar, Reub stepped threateningly towards Clay Brascoe. Clay moved, a sort of stoop which entailed swishing back the right half of his coat so that his hand settled on the polished brown grip of his Colt Peacemaker. 'I told you. You come at me again and you'd better have a gun in your hand.'

Reub stopped. Anger still his controlling force. 'You

think I'm afraid of you?' he asked. He began unbuttoning his own coat.

'No, Reub,' protested Tim Bradall. 'Don't let him goad you.'

'He's not talking about Caroline like that again,' said Reub, spittle spraying the air as his anger forced out the words.

'What have I said that isn't true, Hadley? Your sister's a whore. She sells herself to men.'

'Clay,' cried Caroline, throwing herself against his chest. 'Don't do it.' She turned to face Reub. 'Forget it,' she told him. 'It doesn't matter.'

'Doesn't matter,' repeated Reub. 'What have you become that you can let someone like that talk about you in such a way and say it doesn't matter?'

'Please Reub,' she cried, but Clay Brascoe pushed her away, sent her sprawling in the snow.

'Want to make something of it?' Clay's voice was full of taunt and menace. He smiled, knowing that the smile would be the last straw for Reub Hadley. Reub's hand moved towards his gun. Clay's moved faster. He drew and fired before Reub's weapon was out of its holster. The first shot hit Reub in the centre of his forehead, the second, fired as Reub was falling, was an inch higher and barely an inch to the right. In the silent aftermath the watchers seemed mesmerized by the smoke from Clay Brascoe's Peacemaker as it rose starkly in the icy air.

'You all saw that,' said a satisfied Clay Brascoe. 'He went for his gun first. It was self defence. Him or me. No one can deny that.' He holstered his gun and fastened his jacket.

'That was murder,' said Tim Bradall. 'He didn't have a chance.'

'That's not the way the law will look at it. Self defence.' He smiled, the same smile he'd shown Reub Hadley before he shot him.

Caroline got to her feet and stood over her brother's body. 'Why did you do it, Clay? You didn't have to kill him. He's my brother.'

Tim Bradall looked at the woman he had once called his wife with a mixture of anger and distaste. 'Because he is a killer, Caroline. That's all he knows. That's all that gives him pleasure. If you think he cares for you then you're a fool. He came with us to collect the money that was hidden in your coach. If it was choice between taking you girls to safety or collecting the money, you would still be up there.'

Caroline took the two short steps to Clay Brascoe. She reached out her hand to grasp his arm. 'That's not true, is it, Clay?'

Clay Brascoe brushed her hand away, looked into her eyes and laughed. 'See you in The Red Garter some-time,' he said and walked away.

'If you want my advice,' Tim Bradall said to her, 'you'll do what I told Reub to do. Go home to Fort Worth. Somebody has to tell his parents he's dead. He was staying at the hotel in Wicker. Likely he had some money with him. I guess it's yours now.' He turned to Jess Clarke. 'Help me tie him across his saddle. We'll take him back to Wicker for burial.'

Everyone else was preparing to leave while Tim and Jess busied themselves with the body. Jess had just tied the last knot. He raised his head to tell Tim he'd finished but the words didn't come. Across the trail sat two horsemen, rifles bared and butts resting down on their thighs. Jess nodded in their direction. 'We've got company,' he announced.

CHAPTER FOUR

For long, silent moments the group looked at the two men who were above them on the mountain, not on the trail from Butte to Two Falls Pass but, apparently, on a cross trail, one that came from deeper in the mountain range. Their uncovered faces, an indication that they were no strangers to hardship, almost a challenge to winter's wrath, were dark with hair growth of several days. There was an unnatural similarity in the narrowness of their eyes, the hollowness of their cheeks and the angle at which they held their heads as they watched those below. Their stillness added to their feral appearance, like hawks hovering before swooping on a running rabbit, like cougars gathering on their haunches to spring at a doe, like rattlesnakes poised to strike at the optimum moment. Their naked rifles unsettled everyone.

Eventually, they nudged their horses and picked their way down to the spot where the group had gathered. Only Anne Hames moved, stepping close to Jess Clarke, her left shoulder touching his right arm as though needing the reassurance of his presence, her unwavering

look at the approaching riders telling of her nervousness.

'Looks like you folk have had some trouble.' The first
rider pointed with his rifle at the bundle that was the
body of Reub Hadley lashed to a horse.

'Heard the shots,' explained the second man, his
voice, like his features, identical to those of the other
man. No one doubted they were twins. No one doubted
they were trouble.

'Figured we'd see if we could be of help to anyone,'
said the first rider.

'Yeah, help,' echoed his brother.

Cal Brewster took it upon himself to be spokesman for
the group. 'Nothing anyone can do to help him,' he
moved his head in the direction of the body. 'We're
heading down to Wicker. Hope to get off the mountain
before any more snow falls.'

The first man looked up at the heavy sky, a short blast
of icy wind disturbing his hair and the mane and tail of
his mount. 'Snow's coming now,' he said, his words
emphatic, spoken like he'd lived in the mountains all his
life.

'Yep, coming now,' said his brother, as though his life
had been created for no other reason than to repeat his
brother's words.

'Reckon you're right,' agreed Cal. 'So we'll get underway.'

The first rider shifted the gun that had been resting
on his thigh, lifting it as though moving it to a more com-
fortable position but making a show of the movement so
that no-one would overlook the fact that his rifle was in

his hand and his gloved finger was inside the trigger guard. When he spoke, however, his voice retained the same slow, even tone he'd used from the beginning. 'Thing is,' he said, 'we're seeking some assistance ourselves.'

'Yep,' said his brother who seemed unable to let the other's conversation go unsupported.

'That right,' said Cal.

'Thought perhaps you could help us like we stopped to help you.'

Cal Brewster stepped nearer the horses. A rifle stuck out of a saddle boot, having it in his hands would help quell the unease he now felt. He'd known men like these all along the frontier, men who took what they wanted by whatever means they thought necessary. Road agents, who held up freight wagons and stagecoaches wherever they ran across them, and a party like this one, a party which included a number of women and children, would pose them no problems. Cal hadn't been fooled by the behaviour of the newcomers. He knew they'd inspected every member of the party, not blatantly, but easily, looking round as they talked as though trying to involve everyone in the conversation. Their eyes gliding over everyone with satisfaction, all except Clay Brascoe. In him they recognized a gunman and, that being the case, a possible source of resistance. He'd also seen the second rider's eyes light up when he'd observed Cherokee Lil, Trixie and the other girls. 'In what way can we help?' asked Cal.

The first man turned in his saddle, pointed his rifle back in the direction from which they'd appeared.

'We've got a cabin back there,' he said. 'Got an injured partner. Needs someone to fix him up.'

'What kind of injury?'

'Gunshot. An accident when we were trying to bag some fresh meat.'

Cal rubbed his jaw. 'Need to get him to a doctor. There's a good one in Wicker. You can probably make the journey in a day. '

'That's too far. He's hurt bad,' said the first rider.

'Real bad,' added his brother.

'We need someone to stop the bleeding,' said the first brother, 'and get the bullet out.'

'Can't help you,' said Cal. 'We got our own invalids.' He gestured towards Sarah Fetterman. 'We gotta get Mrs Fetterman to Doc Hames in Wicker as soon as possible.'

Interest in the sudden appearance of the two riders had, for the moment, driven Sarah Fetterman's own discomfort from her mind and with the thought gone, so too had the nausea and headache. Now, apart from the bandage wrapped tight around her forehead, she looked no worse than any of the other travellers; cold, tired and desperate to reach the refuge of a township. 'She looks a whole heap better than our partner. Perhaps whoever fixed her up can do the same for him.'

'Who's looking after him now?'

'Our brother,' said the second brother quickly.

The other one gave him a sharp glance in reprimand. 'We ain't so good at fixing things,' he said. 'Our partner took care of any doctoring we needed, but he can't doctor himself. We need someone. We need someone now.'

106

Since killing Reub Hadley, Clay Brascoe had stood apart from the rest of the party. Even Caroline Bradall hadn't gone near him. Not that that troubled Clay. He revelled in other people's dislike of him – gave him reason to despise them and justify the fights he picked against those who had no desire to draw a gun against him or anyone else. In his opinion, weak people deserved to die. They were no loss to the world. But killing them was the easy part. The fun part was finding a reason to goad them into a fight. He'd really enjoyed getting under the skin of Cimmaron's brother. Strange that it had turned out that way because when they'd sheltered in the cave it was the other one he had expected to kill. Tim Bradall's reluctance to fight Reub Hadley had extended over days which made him an ideal target for Clay's games. But Reub's down-south chivalry and quickness of temper had irritated Clay. In addition, killing him gave a pay-off that killing Tim Bradall wouldn't achieve: it got rid of Cimmaron Kate. He hated the way she clung to him, imagined herself as being something special to him. She was a whore. Her husband knew it, wanted nothing more to do with her and wouldn't raise a finger to protect her. Her brother, on the other hand, had made it clear that he had come in search of her. He would have hopes of saving her from the brutality and disease that was the wages of all the girls who worked in a saloon owned by Duke Ferris. But now her brother was gone and those hopes had gone with him. Clay congratulated himself on the double success – one dead, one irretrievably degraded.

And there were others in the group upon whose lives

he intended to wreak havoc. As he listened to the conversation between Cal Brewster and the two riders a course of action formulated in his mind and it, too, had the potential for producing a double reward. He recognized the two riders. From time to time they'd been in Butte, in company with a third brother and their father. They were the Claytons, known rustlers, highwaymen and bank robbers whose success outside the law was due entirely to the cunning of the father, Thad. It was said of the three brothers that their combined intelligence wouldn't amount to that of a halfwit, but they obeyed their father's instructions without question and were prepared to kill anyone who might prove dangerous to them. The twins were called Ezra and Barney, Ezra being the talker and Barney his echo.

Clay moved slowly towards the horses, keeping his arms crossed as he walked, displaying to the brothers that he wasn't a threat. Nonetheless, even as his conversation with Cal Brewster continued, Ezra kept a careful eye on Clay's advance. Clay paused next to the horse that Anne Hames had ridden, stroked along its flank then lifted its rear leg as though inspecting for stones under the shoe. Satisfied with what he saw he turned his attention to Ezra as though interested in what he had to say. He rested his arm on the horse's back, let his hand rest on the black bag that was tied to the saddle. In idle fashion he drummed his fingers on it until Ezra took notice.

'What's that?' he asked, although his tone suggested he'd already recognized it. 'A doctor's bag?' He scanned the figures standing around, most of their faces muffled with scarves as protection against the cold. 'One of you a doctor?' No one answered. Sam Fetterman shuffled in the snow, a nervous movement which immediately caught Ezra's attention. 'You,' he called. 'Are you the doctor?'

'No. Just travelling west with my family. We'd be the other side of the Bitterroots if the snow hadn't come early.' Nervously, he looked up at the sky. Snow was beginning to fall. His priorities were to get his wife some proper medical attention and to a safe spot where the families could wait out the winter. These two riders looked like the sort of men who thrived on trouble. Not only that, but the rifle that had rested butt down on his thigh was now swinging in an arc towards himself and his family. Sam moved cautiously, trying, impossibly, to get his body between the gunman and each other member of his family.

'Stand still, pilgrim,' said Ezra. 'I want an answer and I want it quick. Which one is the doctor? Point him out.'

Cal Brewster spoke up. 'We ain't gotta doctor with us. Our wagons got caught in a snow slide higher up the mountain and some people from Wicker came to help us. They brought some medical supplies to tend any injuries.'

Ezra Clayton looked down at Cal, unsure if he was telling the truth, his eyes glinting black and menacingly in their narrow slits. Using Sam Fetterman's fear for the safety of his family as a lever to verify Cal's words, he shifted the angle of the rifle so that the eldest Fetterman boy was in its direct line of fire. He held back the hammer with his thumb. 'Is that the truth?' he asked Sam.

Sam Fetterman swallowed, glanced at his boy then chose his words carefully. 'Like Mr Brewster said, no doctor came with them.'

Ezra Clayton held Sam Fetterman's gaze for a moment but could detect no telltale sign that the man was lying. There again, because his hat was pulled down so low on his brow and the collar of his great coat stood up high against his cheeks there was little of Sam's face on view for Ezra to judge that he was telling the truth either. Still, he raised the rifle so that it pointed once more into the air and eased down the hammer with his thumb. He looked around at the other figures gathered in groups of two and three here and there on the snow covered stretch of mountain, their stillness and silence a collective gesture of defiance to him and his brother.

'Yeah, but the bag didn't come up the mountain on its own,' declared Clay Brascoe. 'The young 'un there,' he looked over the horses to where Anne Hames stood alongside Jess Clarke, 'came along to fix up the injured. Done a good job, too, with the woman over there.' He pointed at the bandaged head of Sarah Fetterman.

'You boy,' called Ezra, 'you're a doctor?'

Clay chuckled, the sound full of the meanness of his mind. 'Not a doctor,' he said. 'Not even a boy.'

'What?'

'She's a girl. The daughter of the doctor in Wicker. Dare say she's helped him a lot. Unpaid nurse helping her pappy stitch people together.'

'A girl,' said Ezra, the revelation taking him by surprise. Until now the only medical people he'd encountered had been men, all of them cursing in dim

110

light as they removed lumps of lead or stitched knife cuts and splits in pistol-whipped heads. The other thing they had in common was that they all expected payment for the additional pain they inflicted.

'A girl,' repeated Barney. Even though the many layers of clothes made her prettiness and female form indiscernible, he smiled. The prospect of taking her back to their hideout cabin had nothing to do with providing aid to a wounded man.

'Mount up, girl, you're coming with us,' said Ezra.

'Oh yeah,' murmured Barney, 'coming with us.'

'No she isn't.' Jess's voice rang out loud and clear. 'She's coming back to Wicker with us. She's already got a patient who needs her attention.'

Ezra's rifle swung in an arc again, the barrel pointed unerringly at Jess's chest.

Clay Brascoe reacted instantly, holding up his hand to forbid the discharge of the weapon. Jess Clarke was his to kill just as the girl was his to enjoy. 'No need for violence,' he stated, like he was an ambassador at an Indian peace treaty council. Momentarily, the manner of his intervention duped the travellers into believing he was opposed to Anne going off with the twins. His next words changed their thinking. 'The girl came along with the party to help the injured. Don't seem to matter that the person most in need of her help isn't one of the people we came up here to rescue. These men aren't going to hurt her. They need her to fix up their partner.'

'What about me?' said Sarah Fetterman, anxious at the thought of Anne Hames being at the mercy of the vicious looking twins. 'I need Anne with me.'

'By this time tomorrow you'll be in Wicker. Doc Hames will take care of you.'

'Come on, girl,' Ezra said. 'Our partner needs someone quick.'

'She's not going with you,' Jess Clarke declared again.

Anne Hames grabbed his sleeve as she saw Ezra Clayton begin to raise his rifle again. 'I'll go,' she said, her voice soft but the determination strong. 'Mr Brascoe is right. I came along to offer what help I could. I can be more help going with these men than I would be heading back to Wicker.' Her decision wasn't based solely on the help she might be to their wounded partner but more on the violence she feared would erupt if she didn't go with them. She didn't like the look of the two men but she was only one person, and already unspoken threats had been made to the Fetterman boy and Jess. Clay Brascoe was the only member of their group who looked like he might be a match for them if it came to a gunfight, but Clay's sympathies appeared to be with the newcomers so there was little chance of help from him. Anne was frightened, but couldn't see an alternative to going with the twins.

Jess said, 'I won't let you go,' although how he was going to stop her he didn't know. In his mind he could hear Dan Hathaway, repeating what he'd said in the cave the night before. 'You and me'll just have to take care of her and get her safely home.' If Dan was here he wouldn't let her out of his sight.

'You can't stop me,' said Anne, her head high, the blue of her eyes changed to a watery grey.

'You're right,' said Jess, 'so I'll go with you.'

'Jess!' She gripped his sleeve more tightly.

Although the tenor of this short exchange had been apparent to everyone present, the words themselves had not been overheard because they had been speaking in lowered voices. In the same tone, Jess said, 'You aren't going to object, are you?'

For a moment it seemed as though she would. Behind the scarf that covered the lower part of her face he could see the movement of her lips, as though she had a lot of words to say but couldn't shuffle them into the order she sought. Then the intensity of feeling, the tension that was showing in her eyes, softened. Slowly she shook her head.

Jess turned to Ezra Clayton. 'I'm going with you,' he said.

'No,' said Ezra.

'Anne will need me to help when we get to your cabin.'

'No.' Ezra spoke angrily, prepared to brook no further argument.

Clay Brascoe spoke. 'Perhaps it's not a bad idea,' he said. 'After all, she may need help to find her way back to Wicker.'

Jess wasn't sure he could find the way back either but it seemed like a sound reason for tagging along.

Barney Clayton smirked. 'The way back,' he said to his brother, his meaning clear – no way back existed. Although Ezra was as sure as Barney that there would be no way back for Anne Hames he wasn't prepared to announce the fact or even hint at it. He had caught the drift of Clay Brascoe's thinking, that it was better to deal with the couple away from all these witnesses. If they never turned up in Wicker again, which they wouldn't because once they'd been to the hideout they couldn't be allowed to report its location to the law, then there was nothing to say that they hadn't simply lost their way and frozen to death on the mountain. What Ezra didn't understand was Clay Brascoe's co-operation. Perhaps, he thought, the gunman wanted to become a member of the Clayton gang.

'OK,' Ezra said to Jess. 'Shuck your gunbelt.'

Until that moment Jess had all but forgotten about his father's pistol which was deep in the inside pocket of his long coat. 'I'm not wearing one,' he announced, and to prove it he opened his coat. He hoped they didn't insist that he empty his pockets. He didn't want to give up the gun. In that moment he knew it might be the only thing that got Anne and him out of their clutches because, whoever these men were, he knew they were bad. He also knew they would have to kill him before he allowed any evil to befall Anne.

'Mount up,' Ezra ordered, and soon the Clayton brothers, Anne and Jess were underway.

Those left behind watched as the four riders climbed to the upper trail and disappeared, single file, into a crevice. Snow now fell heavily as they looked around at each other, all except one knowing they should have done more to keep Anne and Jess with them. Cherokee Lil was the first to speak. She spoke to Cal Brewster but looked at Clay Brascoe as she did so, accusing him with her eyes but, in this instance, uncertain of what he was guilty. 'Those twins,' she said, 'they're part of the Clayton gang.'

'Are you sure?'

She nodded. 'Ezra and Barney. I've seen them in Butte.'

'You should have told me sooner. Those young 'uns are in awful trouble.'

'What could you have done?' asked Cherokee Lil. 'They'd've killed you if you'd resisted.'

'We should have done something. Somebody should have done something.' Like Cherokee Lil his gaze settled on Clay Brascoe.

Brascoe said, 'The Clayton boys! Perhaps I shouldn't have encouraged those kids to go with them.' The words were repentant. The flash of satisfaction in his eyes was not.

Cal said, 'Let's get underway. Perhaps we can catch up to the rest of the families before nightfall.'

The gunshot had no echo, the sound deadened by the snow. It came from behind the four riders, from the place they had been a few minutes earlier. Barney twisted in his saddle, the rifle in his hands already pointed along their backtrack in the expectation of pursuit.

'A lame horse,' explained Jess. 'We'd stopped to unload it. They've shot it before moving on.'

Anne Hames looked across at Jess when he uttered the words *moving on*. She recognized the truth of their predicament in those two words – they were alone, at the mercy of unstable and violent men, the distance between themselves and the succour of their community increasing with every step.

'Keep moving,' growled Ezra who was two horse

lengths in front of Anne and Jess, trying to urge some extra pace from his mount, although it was obvious in such conditions that a slow walk was the best they could manage.

Snow was falling heavily and, to his dismay, Jess saw that their tracks were already being lost to the new downfall. He manoeuvred closer to Anne, tried, with a grim smile, to reassure her that all would be well. He felt the weight of the old Colt in his coat pocket bumping against his thigh. He'd never fired it at anything more than tin cans and bottles and he hadn't hit many of those but now it was their lifeline. 'We'll get out of this,' he whispered to Anne, his tone carrying such certainty that, even though he knew she wasn't convinced it was true, he could tell she was grateful for his encouragement. But no sooner were the words out of his mouth than a powerful blow struck him high on his back, across the right shoulder.

Jess grunted with pain and would have fallen from his saddle but for the closeness of Anne's horse to his own.

'Quit talking,' yelled Barney, his rifle raised to deliver another blow.

Anne yelled, her concern divided between holding Jess in his saddle and wanting to lash out at Barney for the unprovoked attack.

'What's going on?' Ezra had wheeled his horse to investigate the commotion behind.

'He struck Jess with his rifle,' complained Anne.

'They were talking,' explained Barney.

'So what? We can't talk?'

'They were whispering, Ez. No doubt they were

making plans to escape.'

'You listen to me,' exploded Anne, fear and anger needing to erupt in a torrent of words, 'I agreed to come with you to treat your partner because he's in need. We are not your prisoners and if you want us to proceed any further you will treat us with a bit more respect.'

'You'll do what you're told,' Ezra snapped at her. He was no less abrupt when he spoke to his brother. 'What's the matter with you? Let them talk. What harm can it do? We need her to get that slug out of Pa. Perhaps we'll need him too. So keep an eye on them but leave them alone.' With that said he turned his horse again and they plodded on.

Ezra was anxious to get back to the cabin. His pa was badly hurt and needed to have the bullet removed as quickly as possible. He knew that for him and his brothers, a future without their pa would be a bleak place. He would be head of the family then because his brothers weren't capable of thinking for themselves. He alone had inherited a modicum of his father's intelligence and cunning. Consequently, they would look to him to plan and provide for them as their father had always done. It was a task he neither wanted nor felt capable of fulfilling. Barney had never had any sense. Violence was his solution to everything. Just now, Ezra thought, he could have shot the boy with the same lack of compunction as he had hit him with the butt end of his gun. The decision had probably been made by the way he was holding the rifle at the moment he chose to intervene. And Algy, the youngest, was no better, perhaps even more simple than Barney. Their only ability was with a gun. Not that they were fast on the draw but they used them willingly and accurately. In vain, Ezra clicked his tongue, but any hope of coaxing a bit more effort from his horse was lost in deep snow. He wished the cabin was closer.

For ten minutes or so Barney didn't allow his eyes to stray from the couple in front. Keep an eye on them, Ez had said, but that soon became a wearisome task. The way the lad leaned forward over his saddle horn, favouring the shoulder that had taken the blow from the rifle butt, amused Barney, but the lad seemed to be keeping the pain to himself, not rubbing his shoulder or complaining about it to the girl. She had cast one or two glances at the lad but was getting nothing in return. She kept her gaze forward and everyone rode in silence. Barney thought about the girl, thought of the fun he would have when she'd finished doctoring his pa.

Anne brushed her leg against Jess's to attract his attention. 'How much further to their cabin?' she whispered.

'No idea. Perhaps not far.' He fell silent for a moment not wanting to give Barney any cause to repeat his assault. 'We have to get away from them,' he said, moving his lips as little as possible. 'If they get us to the cabin they'll kill us.'

The same thought had been running through Anne's mind. 'What do we do?'

Jess felt again for the gun in his pocket. It gave him momentary hope but he knew he wasn't a gunman, couldn't hope to outgun two desperadoes for whom gunplay figured large in their lives. 'I'm not sure,' he confessed, 'but if we don't get away soon the snow is going to cover the tracks and it will be more difficult to

118

find our way back. Perhaps we can distract them,' he suggested. 'If we can get them off their horses at least one of us might have a chance of escape.'

Anne Hames didn't like the suggestion that only one of them might be able to escape but under the circumstances it was impossible to argue. Jess had turned away from her, was throwing a quick glance over his shoulder. Barney was watching them, trying to catch their conversation but not making any attempt to draw closer. Clearly, Jess thought, he was in awe of his brother and wasn't going to do anything that would upset him. Nonetheless, Jess allowed his horse to drift slightly away from Anne's so that Barney wouldn't watch them so intently.

Another hundred yards of high stepping through deep snow brought another nudge from Anne. Jess looked across. She had loosened the thongs that held the medical bag to the saddle, was holding it in place with her left hand and indicated that she could let it fall whenever necessary. That would cause a diversion. They would have to stop. Someone would have to climb down to collect the bag because it held the tools she needed to cut out the bullet.

'When I yell,' he whispered, 'just ride away. Follow our trail and don't stop until you catch up with the others.'

'What about you?' Alarm showed in her eyes.

'I'll join you as soon as I'm able.' She shook her head, it was the slightest of movements but carried the full weight of her opposition. Jess ignored it. 'Don't look back,' he whispered, 'and don't stop.'

She wanted to shout at him, tell him she wouldn't do

it. Wouldn't let him sacrifice himself especially when there was no real plan and no guarantee of success, but he'd turned away, begun fiddling with the small hat that now carried a layer of snow an inch thick, and hunched his shoulders as though the cold had penetrated his clothing and was hurting his bones. He took a deep breath, fixed his eyes on Anne, looked her square in the eyes as though trying to absorb every detail of the one part of her face he could see so that he would remember them forever, then nodded his head. Now was the time.

When the bag fell it almost came as a surprise to Anne herself. She had been reluctant to proceed with the plan. She didn't know what Jess intended doing other than place himself in danger so that she could get away, but even if that part was a success there was no guarantee that she would ever get off the mountain alive. She had turned in the saddle to examine the trail they'd left behind. It was clear enough at the moment but even if she made it to the point where Reub Hadley had been killed there would be little daylight and it was still a long way down to Two Falls Pass. With her mind concerned with the possible consequences of Jess Clarke's plan, the bag slipped from her hand.

'Oh!' She shouted and reined her horse to a halt.

'What's happening?' Ezra called back before looking round and stopping.

Jess and Barney too had reined in beside Anne.

'The doctor's bag has come loose,' Jess informed Ezra. 'I'll get it.' He climbed down, walked around the horses and reclaimed the bag from the deep snow. 'Hope nothing in here is damaged,' he said, almost conversationally. He opened the bag and peered inside. 'No broken bottles,' he told Anne. 'The snow must have cushioned the fall.'

'Good,' said Anne, unsure of what was going to happen next.

'Hurry up,' shouted Ezra, turning his horse again, anxious to be under way.

Jess busied himself retying the bag to the saddle straps then walked round behind Anne's mount and in front of Barney's keeping his eyes on the rifle which Barney held in his right hand. Then he struck.

From the bag, unseen, Jess had removed a scalpel and had slid it up his sleeve. Now, with Barney's concentration centred on the trail ahead, peering towards a looming crest as though the landmark was missing a special feature, Jess stuck the scalpel into the top of the horse's leg. It screamed, reared, eyes rolled and it screamed again as its hoofs struck the ground. It rolled onto its side, away from Jess who, with agility, sprang towards the falling animal. Before Barney could react, Jess wrenched the rifle from his hands and swiped it across his brow, spreading him senseless in the snow. In almost the same movement and thinking only to put the weapon beyond Barney's reach, Jess flung the gun over the edge of the mountain.

'Go, Anne!' he yelled and slapped the flank of her horse as he ran past it. He didn't look at her, instead his eyes were focused on Ezra Clayton. In response to the commotion, Ezra was turning his horse to the left and trying to pull his rifle from its scabbard. Jess ran to the right, keeping himself behind Ezra, keeping him off balance so that he could get close enough to grab him. Jess was a strong lad; he knew that if he could get a handful of coat he could haul Ezra out of the saddle. He was also confident enough to believe he could get the best of Ezra in a fist fight. But even as he was reaching up to fill his hands with Ezra's coat the voice of Dan Hathaway tried to force its way into his thinking. He knew it was a warning, a reprimand, something he should have done but hadn't. *If the time comes that you have to kill him then don't hesitate. Just do it. Some men need killing.* Dan had been talking about Clay Brascoe when he'd given that advice but it was just as true, he supposed, about these brothers. Killing, however, wasn't a natural part of Jess's make-up. He now realized he'd acted too hastily, without a proper course of action in mind. After knocking out one brother he should have been prepared to shoot the other, which would have left Anne and him free to make their way off the mountain together. He'd had the opportunity, had had a rifle in his hands and Ezra at his mercy, but he'd thrown it away, and even though he still had his father's old pistol, his chance of shooting Ezra had probably slipped from his grasp. The gun was deep in his coat pocket, not easily retrieved even if he'd been a more experienced gunfighter. Any attempt to reach it would result in his relinquishing the advantage he currently held. Even if he was able to draw it and fire first there was no guarantee that he would hit his target. Ezra, on the other hand, was clearly accustomed to handling guns, capable of killing with one shot. The situation left Jess with no alternative; he could only pursue the strategy he'd already undertaken: attempt to confuse and unhorse Ezra.

Fortune, at that moment, was favouring Jess Clarke. Or perhaps it was his tactic of keeping Ezra off balance by swerving to the opposite side of his horse whenever he tried to turn. The underfoot conditions were not conducive to agile footwork for a big animal and more than once the horse slipped on the icy ground. Its awkward movement also made it difficult for Ezra to remove his Winchester so, by the time Jess gripped his coat, the gun was still not in his hand. Jess hauled him from the saddle flinging a punch at his jaw as he did so. Ezra went down, cursing, scrabbling to his knees as Jess advanced towards him. Ezra was scrawny, his arms were long and he'd brawled in barrooms from Butte to El Paso. He knew more about dirty fighting than Jess knew of the stock on his father's farm.

But Jess surprised him, launching himself at Ezra when he was still five strides away, his left shoulder smashing into Ezra's chest, winding him, knocking him flat on his back again. Jess sat astride his opponent's chest and crashed a huge fist against his jaw, numbing his hand as much as he stunned Ezra. He looked up then, could see Anne riding back along the trail and he felt a moment of triumph. It was short lived. Ezra heaved his body, throwing Jess to one side and immediately swinging a long, right-arm punch at his head. Jess blocked it with his left arm but couldn't do anything about the short cross with the left hand that landed flush on his jaw. Staggered by that, he rolled away from Ezra before another punch could be thrown. Both men got to their feet and came together in a wresting grip, shoulder to shoulder, heads crossed. Ezra used his knee, sinking it deep and fiercely into Jess's groin. Jess gasped and sank to his knees. Ezra smashed a fist into his face, rendering him almost unconscious.

Barney, legs unsteady and blood leaking from a gash on his brow, approached. He kicked Jess in the stomach and again in the back. He began unbuttoning his coat, reaching inside for the pistol he carried on his hip. At that moment a shot rang out. It came from the trail ahead, from the crest that had held Barney's attention when Jess had begun his attack. A man seemed to be dancing there. His legs coming high off the ground, knees bent, and his arms waving in the air, hands at either end of a rifle. He wore a tattered hat and a long coat which flapped as he gesticulated to the twins.

'Algy,' said Barney. 'He's gone crazy being alone up here for a day.'

'He's not alone,' said Ezra, worried, 'he's looking after Pa. Come on. I think he needs us.'

Barney had his pistol in his hand, the hammer cocked, and he lowered the barrel, pointing it at Jess's head. A warning shout from his brother distracted him from pulling the trigger. When he raised his head it was to see a horse, fast approaching and not six strides from him. Instinctively, he threw himself backwards, out of its path, as its rider jumped down to lay herself across Jess Clarke's stricken form.

'Don't shoot.' Anne Hames pleaded. She lifted Jess's head and cradled it in her arms. 'I still need him.'

The grim expression on Barney's face gave Anne little hope of saving Jess's life. Ezra's expression was little

better but he wasn't yet ready to throw away any opportunity to save his father. If the girl said she needed the
young fellow to help her then so be it. 'But you'd better
get that slug out of Pa,' he warned.

'Then can we go? she asked.

'We'll decide that when the old man's back on his
feet.'

Barney grinned. 'On his feet,' he said and Anne knew
she had only postponed their execution.

'What about him?' Barney asked, toeing the unconscious figure on the ground.

'Throw a rope around him,' ordered Ezra, 'and drag
him up to the cabin.'

CHAPTER FIVE

On the way to Two Falls Pass, Dan Hathaway had spoken of the presence of long forsaken shacks scattered amongst the mountains. They had been the rickety homes of gold and silver prospectors enduring hardship in the constant expectation of riches, assemblies of timber which, in the main, provided little protection and less comfort. At first appearance, the best thing that could be said about the one in which the Clayton family had taken refuge was that it was still standing. However, considering its location on a broad slope which ran down to a chasm that dropped three hundred feet to the valley below, it was a minor miracle that it hadn't completely blown away in a storm many years ago. It had no windows and a flimsy door that chattered in its frame like a medicine man's rattle when the wind blew. And when the wind blew, draughts seeped through the gaps between every adjoining plank. To combat these, animal skins had been nailed over many parts of the walls but their effectiveness was limited.

It consisted of only one room, adequate accommodation for a single man who toiled from sunup to beyond

126

sundown. A table and stools were pushed into one corner and a bed ran the length of one side. A cupboard, cobbled together with the same degree of craftsmanship as had been put into the building of the shack, stood opposite the bed. Its saving grace was a pot-bellied, wood burning stove which, on this day, was hard at work.

Momentarily, Anne Hames welcomed the warmth inside the shack. It seemed, until the door was opened, that she had been on the mountain forever, that the chill of the icy wind inhabited her body. The warmth brought with it a sense of security, a reason to banish the morbid thoughts that had occupied her since the parting of the ways beside Harv Prescott's dead horse.

Then the smell assailed her senses and the horror of her situation engulfed her again. It was a foul smell. A smell like offal. A smell which wasn't improved by the heat in the room. The cause of it was the drying pool of blood on the floor near the bed and the blood-soaked sheet that covered the man who lay there.

'That's Pa,' Ezra told her, because there was no longer any need for pretence. Even if she discovered they were the wanted Clayton gang it wouldn't do her any good because she was never going to leave this place. 'Get that bullet out of him. Fix him up. We can't stay here long. Got to ride tomorrow.'

'I'm not a doctor,' Anne reminded him. 'Even if I was,' she added standing over the man in the bed, 'he won't be on a horse for a long time.' She observed the greyness of her patient's face, noted the amount of blood that had already been lost and knew that she couldn't save his life. The man was on the threshold of eternity as she spoke and that knowledge scared her. When he stepped out of the world she and Jess would be close behind.

'Tomorrow,' said Ezra. 'Get that bullet out of him and we'll ride tomorrow.' Anne detected a wildness in his eyes that hadn't been present when he and his brother had first appeared but she wasn't sensible of the thoughts that had occupied his mind on the way back to the shack. Responsibility brought worries and he knew that upon his decisions depended the safety of his brothers and father. After robbing the bank at Missoula the law would be after them and after today's encounter he couldn't take his family to Wicker. Even if those people didn't know who they were, Barney and he could never set foot in that town. They would be recognized as the men who took away the young 'uns and, if the townsfolk caught them, they would lynch them. Ezra rued the fact that he hadn't killed the rest of that party. Doubtless a search party would be raised as soon as they reached town and told of the encounter, so travelling on couldn't be delayed. In the morning they would head south, away from the winter snow.

Hands on hips to demonstrate a determination she neither felt nor was in a position to uphold, Anne Hames looked sternly around the room. 'If I'm to get started I need Jess in here. Where is he?'

Ezra flung open the door and yelled at his brothers. 'That's enough, Barney. Bring him in. There's work to do.' Moments later the brothers came in hauling Jess on the end of the rope that had dragged him the hundred yards from his short lived revolution. Barney gave the rope a sudden, violent tug which catapulted Jess through the doorway into a collision with the table and stools in the corner. There was blood on his face. His lips were cut, a long slit had opened over his left eye and there was an ugly, uneven gash across the bridge of his nose.

Anne knelt beside him, removed the loop of the rope that had pinioned his arm while Barney and Algy had taken turns to punch him, and discarded it under the bed so that she could help him to his feet. He couldn't straighten because to do so sent a searing pain through his groin. Anne glared at Ezra, prepared to vent her anger at him, but realized the hopelessness of such a course of action. 'Sit down,' she told Jess, upstanding one of the stools into which he had collided. 'I need my bag,' she said, 'if someone can get it for me.'

Ezra despatched Algy to the job. He was a lanky lad with facial features not unlike the twins. It was clear they were brothers but the younger didn't have the same sinewy toughness of the others. Not physically nor even mentally. He had a simpleness of mind which showed in his expressions and behaviour. He grinned when spoken to by his elder brothers and did whatever they asked of him. He went out of the shack with Ezra's command ringing in his ears: 'Don't open the bag.'

'I'll need some water,' ordered Anne. 'Boiled.' Ezra delegated the job of boiling water to Barney. 'And we'll have to move your father into the middle of the room where there's more light,' continued Anne. 'He should be lying on something firm.' The last was merely a thought spoken aloud. She knew it made no difference to the older man what he was lying on because he wasn't going to survive the night no matter whether she tried to remove the bullet or not. She was amazed by her lack of concern for the fate of the man and wondered if such detachment would make her a good or bad doctor. Mentally she shook off such thoughts. At that moment her only concern was her own survival. And, of course, the survival of Jess Clarke.

'There's the table,' Ezra said.

Anne dismissed the suggestion. 'Not big enough,' she said. 'We'll get by with him on the bed.'

Algy returned clutching the doctor's bag that had been tied to Anne's saddle. He held it with both hands, tight against his chest, proving to Ezra that he'd obeyed his order. The bag hadn't been opened.

A paraffin lamp was found and lit and stood on the cupboard against the wall. Then the four men each took a corner of the bed and lifted it to the middle of the room so that the little daylight which was available and the unstable flame from the paraffin lamp would be as much help as possible to Anne. As they moved the bed Algy stumbled, tripping over something that had been lying underneath. Ezra cursed him, looked down to see what had obstructed his brother and the anger fled from his face. 'Put those saddle-bags in the corner,' he told Barney when the bed was positioned where Anne determined.

Standing over her patient, gently raising the blood-stained shirt so that she could see the extent of the damage caused by the lead lump that had torn into his body, Anne's wrist was suddenly and tightly gripped by Pa Clayton's hand. A slight gasp escaped her and her initial response was to try to pull her hand free. She looked at his face. The eyes were open, not wide but with a glass-like stare that made her wonder how much he could see. 'I'm going to remove the bullet,' she told him. His features were expressionless, free of pain, free of care. His grip on her wrist tightened, hurting Anne until she was forced to try to prise his fingers apart. Eventually, it required Jess's help to escape his hold. Ezra Clayton drew close, grinned and expressed pride in his father, that, even with a slug inside him, he wasn't one to miss an opportunity to hold on to a pretty girl.

Whatever Thad Clayton thought he was holding on to, Anne was sure he didn't think it was her. Life was drain-ing from him quickly so she needed to begin the operation straight away, while the brothers knew their father was still alive. Ezra, she determined, was so eager to get his father fit to ride again that he seemed to have dismissed the possibility of him dying. Even the pallid, blood-drained countenance hadn't registered the immi-nence of death. Barney hadn't looked at his father since entering the shack. He wouldn't be concerned until Ezra was concerned. If Ezra said his father would be ready to ride tomorrow then Barney would believe and echo those words.

It was Algy, Anne thought, who, despite his simple-mindedness, sensed something dramatic about his father's condition. His behaviour, when she'd first observed him on the ridge as they approached the shack, had been little short of frantic. First waving and dancing to attract their attention then moving towards the shack as if beckoning them to follow. Then returning to the crest to repeat the performance. But his mental powers were severely limited. He seemed devoid of any ability to convert the concern he felt into words, a handicap which was increased by a childlike concentration span. As soon as Barney had hauled Jess into view on the end of rope, Algy had reverted to his normal violent character and had alternated with Barney holding and punching their prisoner. But now, back in the shack, unless obeying his brother's instruction, he showed a reluctance to get close to the spot where his father lay.

While they waited for the water to boil, Anne Hames attended to the cuts on Jess Clarke's face. She hoped to tell him what she planned to do but the presence of all three brothers made a private conversation impossible.

Jess whispered a question. 'Why did you come back?'

She gazed at him, her expression serious, as though he shouldn't have needed to ask the question. She said, 'Why should I leave you? You wouldn't leave me.' Then out loud she told Ezra Clayton that there were too many people in the room, that he and his brothers would have to wait outside while she and Jess worked.

'It's snowing,' he said, 'and freezing.'

There's not enough light,' she said. 'You'll have to get out so that I can see what I'm doing.'

'Get on with it,' he told her, turning his back and joining his brothers at the table in the corner where they were beginning a card game. There was a finality in his tone which told her that further argument was useless.

As her father had instructed when she'd assisted him in the past, she dropped the implements she would need in a bowl of boiling water. Then she cut open his shirt and began to wash his chest. The hole was enormous and jagged and Anne suspected that it was the exit hole, that the man had been shot in the back either at close quarters or by a rifle shot. With Jess's help she lifted him and saw that a tremendous amount of blood saturated the back of his shirt and the bed on which he lay.

She glanced up at Jess, tried without words to convey the message that she wanted him to play along with what she said and did. Unable to comprehend her intentions, he did the only thing that seemed sensible. He remained silent.

Anne made a big show of extracting a brown bottle from the doctor's bag which stood on the floor where the bed had been. With it she had a roll of bandage and some thin, lint cloth.

'What's that?' asked Ezra, eyeing the bottle with suspicion.

'Morphine,' Anne told him. 'He'll sleep while I get the bullet out and for a few hours after. It'll dull the pain when he wakes up.'

'He'll be able to ride, though? Tomorrow?'

'All I can say is he'll sleep through the night. Perhaps he'll be able to make his own decision in the morning.' As she turned back to the bed she saw Thad Clayton's arm slide off the trunk of his body where it had lain and lie with a heavy finality by his side. His jaw slid open and a hushed rush of air left his body. Anne quickened her step hoping that none of the brothers had recognized the sound of their father's dying breath. She lifted his hand, felt for a pulse and found nothing.

'Hold that pad over his nose and mouth,' she told Jess,

'and pour four drops onto it from the bottle. 'I'll tell you when more is needed.' She looked him in the eyes and mouthed, 'He's dead.'

Anne worked hard, pretending with probes and scalpels, cleaning and stitching the flesh and finally swathing the dead man's chest with bandage. The smell of morphine hung sickly and heavily in the small room. Jess opened the door but the snow blustered in and the wind caused the paraffin lamp to flicker. The brothers protested in unison.

'Your father will sleep for some hours,' declared Anne. 'Don't disturb him. I'll attend to him during the night.'

Barney lifted his eyes from his cards and met those of Ezra. He mumbled a few words. Algy laughed in his simple way and looked across at Anne. 'Barney says he'll attend to you during the night.'

'Shut up, Algy,' said Ezra.

Jess moved away from the doorway, closer to Anne, silently offering a protection that he had no idea how to implement. He collected their coats that had been cast on the floor while they'd pretended to treat a gunshot wound on a dead man. Anne's plan, he realized, was just to give them more time, though he wasn't sure what relief she expected it to bring. There was no hope of rescue; the rest of the party would be well on the way to Two Falls Pass. No one would organize a search for them until they were back in Wicker. And if Anne was hoping to make an escape attempt during the night when the brothers were asleep, it seemed to have little hope of success. They would be afoot and by now the snow would have wiped out all trace of the trail that would lead them off the mountain. In any case, he expected the brothers to guard them through the night. Even if they didn't, the fact that they were all in one room meant that any movement would almost certainly disturb their sleep. Escape was impossible. No, they had to face the fact that, even if the dead man wasn't discovered before morning, their usefulness to the brothers was now at an end and their death was imminent. Anything that antagonized any of the brothers could cause the trigger to be pulled.

Anne sat against the wall where the bed had been. The room was warm but the draughts from the ill fitting timbers caused her to hug her knees. Jess draped her coat around her shoulders and did the same with his own coat around his own shoulders. It was obvious that Anne had chosen this spot because it was the furthest point from the card playing brothers with the bed between, but it seemed to be the point where the wind blew most strongly through the gaps. A bearskin that had been attached to the wall fluttered with the draught. Jess put his hand against it to still it and discovered that the wood behind it was insecure. Either it hadn't been well fixed in the first place or something had struck the shack and caused some damage. As he shuffled against the wall, hoping his weight would retain the bearskin in its proper place and reduce the draught into the room, he felt the thump of the pistol in his pocket as it struck his hip. Once again the thought of drawing it and shooting it out with the brothers entered his head but once again his inexperience held his hand. His only chance of success would be to shoot them before they were able to draw their own weapons. But he wasn't fast and he wasn't accurate and to fail would leave Anne at their mercy. Still, he told himself, it might be the only chance they had. He shuffled again, pulling out from under him the rope that had been used to drag him to the shack.

Ezra pushed back his chair, stood and contemplated the form of his father. For a moment, Anne feared he was going to cross to the bed. Thad Clayton's face was already tinged with the cold greyness of death and any close examination would soon put the lie to her declaration that he slept. She, too, stood, her eyes fixed on Ezra, daring him to disobey her instruction that his father was not to be disturbed. The look in her eyes was a challenge to Ezra. He took a step forward. She pushed back her shoulders and walked around the bed until she stood in front of him, barring any further advance toward his father.

'Did you want something?' she asked.

Ezra looked down at her, the uncertainty of a future without his father still dominant in his mind. 'Still sleeping?' he asked.

'He'll sleep for hours,' she said.

'Did you get the bullet out?'

Anne couldn't understand how Ezra could think there was a lump of lead in his father. He had to know there was a hole in the front and back of his body, but there again, she thought, he had to know from the amount of blood the man had lost that survival was unlikely yet seemed unwilling to acknowledge such a possibility. 'There wasn't a bullet,' she told him. 'It went straight through.'

'So we'll be able to put him on a horse tomorrow?'

'Yes,' said Anne, picturing the old man tied across the saddle, 'you'll be able to put him on a horse.'

Satisfied with Anne's words he turned back to his brothers. 'Algy, make some coffee,' he ordered, then sat down again.

Barney had been listening to his brother's conversation with Anne. 'Done all she can now for Pa,' he said softly to his brother, his eyes following Anne as she returned to stand near Jess at the far side of the bed. 'Reckon it's time for her to do something for me.'

'Forget it,' growled Ezra. 'She's gotta nurse Pa through the night. Gotta get him fit to ride tomorrow. I don't want anything to interfere with that.'

'Aw, come on, Ez. We got more money out of that bank in Missoula than we've ever had before. We need a bit of fun to celebrate.'

'You can celebrate all you want when we get clear of this country. No good having all that money and getting caught by a posse before we have the chance to spend it.' Barney's gaze and thoughts were still fixed on the girl. 'Did you and Algy take care of the horses?'

Barney shook his head.

'Well do it now.'

'Algy's making coffee.'

'You don't need Algy's help. The critters'll be pleased to get into that shed. Unsaddle them and feed them some oats. Won't take you long.'

Grumbling, Barney went to the flimsy door of the shack and opened it. A flurry of snow blew into the room, carried by an icy wind. 'I'll freeze out there,' complained Barney.

'So will the horses if we don't get them sheltered. And we need healthy horses in the morning.' But Ezra had some sympathy with his twin brother. The weather had worsened since they'd got back to the shack. He considered sending Algy out with Barney but the younger Clayton's mind was already occupied with coffee making duties and he knew from experience that it didn't pay to load Algy with two tasks. He looked at Jess and Anne. They had no means of escape and no place to go if they did leave the shack. 'Algy,' he called, 'keep an eye on those two while Barney and I look after the horses. If they try to escape you can shoot them.' Ezra added that last sentence more to deter Anne and Jess but having uttered it he wondered what confusion it would excite in his brother's mind.

Even before the shack door closed, Algy had drawn his six-gun, pointed it first at Jess then at Anne but it was apparent that he had no idea why he needed to do so. Ezra's words, shoot them, was the instruction uppermost in his mind and to obey that instruction he needed his gun in his hand.

Algy's expression of bewildered excitement worried Jess who stood close to Anne. When he'd been tied and beaten it was this brother who had inflicted most damage to him, his punches and kicks delivered with unbridled venom, as though he had no appreciation of violence or suffering, his satisfaction arising from Jess's grunts and grimaces as agony was inflicted. Even so, alone with only one brother, Jess knew that this was an opportunity to escape, and even though they had no plan of where to go or how to get there he knew it was an opportunity they must take. 'Can I have some coffee?' he asked as he took a single step towards the pot-bellied stove.

Algy reacted by swinging the gun to point at Jess's chest.

Anne, catching a sign from Jess and figuring he had devised some plan of escape, moved in the opposite direction, towards the bed, around it and across to the door. 'I'm not going to run away,' she told him. 'I just want to see where the horses are stabled.'

Algy's movements were like little jumps as he tried to cover both Jess and Anne. The girl was getting close to the door and Ezra had told him to shoot them if they tried to escape, but the other one was still talking about coffee so he couldn't mean to go anywhere. He looked at Jess who hadn't moved any further but who still gesticulated for coffee from the pot on the stove. Anne had a hand on the door, appeared to be going to open it. She was the one who was going to escape. Algy concentrated on her. Anne smiled at him, nervously, spoke again of her concern for the horses, wanted to be sure that they would be fit for travel in the morning. He motioned with the gun for her to move away from the door, thought about walking forward, getting closer to her, but the next second he was fighting for his life.

While Algy's full concentration was on Anne, Jess could have withdrawn the pistol from the pocket of his greatcoat, stepped close enough to eradicate any fear of failure and shot the youngest Clayton. But a gunshot would have brought the twins running and Jess hoped to gain some headway before Algy's body was discovered. He and Anne needed all the time they could get if they were to have any chance of evading capture and certain death. So instead of using his pistol he elected to use a tool with which he had proven ability. In one movement he scooped up the rope that had earlier been used to bind him and flipped the loop over Algy's head. Before the simple-minded outlaw realized the significance of the rope around his neck it had been pulled tight and he had been jerked off his feet. Reacting with the inborn instinct of self preservation, Algy dropped his guns so that his fingers could scrabble at the tightening noose, desperately trying to free the constriction at his throat.

But Jess was strong. His initial pull had toppled Algy and while the outlaw struggled with hands and feet, Jess dragged him across the floor until he was able to use a bedpost like a saddle-horn and wrap the rope twice around it to secure it in place. 'Anne,' he called, his voice, husky and low. 'Take the rope.'

The sight of the outlaw struggling for his life had momentarily shocked Anne. Watching Algy choke was a horrible experience but she knew it was him or them and she shook off the repulsion she was feeling. Thinking to put the weapon beyond the outlaw's reach, she kicked the dropped pistol under the bed then ran to join Jess.

'Pull on the rope,' he told her and while she took over the task he had started he dropped onto the floor and grabbed Algy's legs. There was a dual reason for doing this. First, to suppress the noise caused by his boot heels as they drummed a desperate rhythm in his struggle for survival. The other was that pulling on his legs would speed up his death and Jess was conscious that every second was vital.

When Algy's struggle was over, when his organs and muscles had ceased to function, Jess cast a look at Anne. Her jaw trembled but Jess knew it was due to the strength she'd expended by hauling on the rope. 'Quick,' he said, 'Fasten your coat and grab your hat. We've got to get out of here.' While he talked, he removed the loop of the lasso from Algy's neck, unwound the tail from the bedpost and formed it into a coil large enough to slip over his head and one shoulder. He hadn't seen his own, small hat since arriving at the shack so he picked up one that could have been Algy's or his father's. It was dirty and a little too large, but he needed some protection for his head out there on the open mountain.

Anne was heading for the door when Jess called her back. 'This way,' he said, 'and bring one of those stools.' Anne didn't know what he was planning but obeyed without question. Jess was tearing one side of the old bearskin away from the wall of the shack. Behind, as he'd suspected, the wood was cracked and damp and would be easily broken. He grasped a plank and began to push against it. 'I hope the twins don't hear,' he said, and almost simultaneously, the wood gave way.

When the hole was wide enough, he pushed Anne through then followed himself. From the outside he reached back into the room and dragged the stool up to the wall to keep the bearskin in place. Perhaps it wouldn't work, Jess thought, but tracks in the snow would be easy to follow so it was essential to fool Ezra and Barney as long as possible.

The back of the shack was no more than twenty yards from the rock face of the mountain and off to the right was a second building, the place where the horses were being stabled, where, even now, a faint light showed while Ezra and Barney worked.

'That's where we need to be,' whispered Jess. 'If we could get to the horses and take them all with us we'd perhaps have a chance.'

'But we can't wait here,' said Anne. She pointed at the trail they'd made in the snow. 'They'll easily find us.'

Jess pointed down the slope, towards the ridge they'd come across, the ridge on which they'd first seen Algy. 'There is cover over there,' he said. 'A few trees and boulders. Perhaps we'll be able to find somewhere to hideout until we get the opportunity to come back for the horses.' It meant coming round to the front of the shack but Anne nodded her agreement. No other solution offered itself to her. 'Keep low,' advised Jess, 'and if they come out the stable, fall flat in the snow. Now that the light's going they might not see us.'

His words were partly prophetic. It was no longer snowing as they skirted the area around the shack, keeping close to the face of the mountain so that their footsteps were less easy to see. Anne led the way, Jess stepping where she had trodden to lessen, even further, the evidence of their departure. They were edging towards the ridge, keeping clear of the broad slope in front of the shack that angled down to the chasm. Slipping there, Jess guessed, could be fatal. Every second or third stride he threw a glance over his shoulder, wary of the emergence of the twins from the stable. Ezra's voice suddenly carried over the open stretch of mountain and the pair dropped flat.

A dusting of snow arose with the force of their fall and it was that which caught Barney's attention. 'What was that?' he asked his brother, pointing to where the risen snow still hovered in the air.

'Snow falling off a tree,' suggested Ezra.

Barney wasn't convinced and his curiosity aroused his brother's suspicion. Posse, Ezra thought, though how they could have found the hideout in this weather amazed him. 'Let's get inside,' he said to Barney because his rifle was propped in the corner beside the table.

Unlike Ezra who could hold facts and analyze them with the same sort of rapidity as their father, though not with the same accuracy, Barney needed confirmation of information before being able to accept it. Unaware of Ezra's supposition that the movement in the snow was caused by posse men, he sauntered forward a few steps, peering at the point to which he'd been attracted by the powder of snow.

Then Ezra's voice bellowed from within the shack. 'It's them. They've gone. They've killed Algy.'

Barney half turned, unsure that he believed what Ezra had said but in an instant, all doubt was gone. Ezra's voice had carried to Jess and Anne lying motionless in the snow and Jess knew that their only hope now rested in his ability with a gun. He took the pistol from the deep inner pocket of his coat. 'When I begin shooting get over the ridge and as far away as you can.' He lifted his head and fired once, twice and had the satisfaction of seeing Barney fall on his face in the snow. He knew he hadn't hit his target but the bullets must have passed close enough to cause Barney some concern.

Anne was almost over the ridge when he looked round. At a crouch he ran after her, trying to run in a zigzag course but the deep snow made such a manoeuvre difficult. However, it was effective enough to make Barney's two answering pistol shots go harmlessly by. Then, as he reached the top of the ridge, something tugged his coat at the shoulder and toppled him over the edge. The deep, rumbling echo of a rifle shot told him that Ezra was hot on his heels.

He gained his feet and ran on, eyes straining for a sight of Anne in front and in fear of a sight of the pursuing twins. Ahead there were trees that offered some cover and he had no alternative but to head for them. He glanced back. Barney was following his trail. Pistol in hand, he had gained the top of the ridge. A lump of bark flew out of the tree inches above his head and the rifle shot carried after it. Jess needed no further incentive to begin running again. He ran hard, trying to keep as many trees as possible between himself and his pursuers, but they were sparse in number and great in distance between.

Another shot zinged off a tree ahead and Jess stooped lower as he ran, trying to make himself a smaller target, hoping that, with his eyes mainly focused on the ground, he would not run into a tree or a low slung branch that would knock him off his feet. It was running thus that almost led to disaster. Dodging between two trees and simultaneously glancing over his shoulder for signs of pursuit, he'd suddenly realized he'd step out onto the rim of a precipice and that one more step would take him over the edge. He halted suddenly, teetered on the edge then regained his balance. Behind him he could hear Barney, coming quickly, angrily, anxious to kill the man who had slain his brother.

Then Jess heard a welcome sound. Off to his left Anne whispered his name. In an instant an idea occurred to him. Swiftly, he uncoiled the rope that had been across his chest. He secured the loop around the base of a tree and threw the other end to Anne, indicating that she needed to pull it taut when his pursuer reached that spot.

Jess stood tall, made himself a target and, when Barney emerged from between two trees less than a dozen yards away, he fired two shots hoping to hit his man but turning and running in case, as he expected, he missed. He ran forward but only for a couple of strides before veering to his right, balancing precariously on the rim above the chasm.

Barney charged forward, firing his pistol, certain that Jess had run straight ahead. When he passed between the two trees Anne pulled on the rope and it caught Barney just above the ankles. He toppled forward, grasped for something solid to break his fall but he was over the edge of the mountain and falling before the realization of doom entered his mind.

Ezra heard the long, fading scream and knew that he had no more brothers.

Although Ezra's whereabouts were unknown to them, Jess and Anne were reluctant to go any further from the shack. They agreed that the horses were still essential if they were to get off the mountain and they needed to get back to them as soon as possible. Retracing their steps didn't seem a good idea. Ezra, with his rifle, could pick them off from a distance and Jess only had two bullets left in his pistol. He thought that the rim on which they now stood probably led back around to the slope in front of the cabin and, although under the current conditions such a journey was not without risk, it seemed their best hope of reaching the horses unobserved. So they began, Jess leading the way, testing every footstep, wary that any mistake might cause them to plummet to their death.

The chase over the ridge and through the trees had taken no more than five minutes, the climb back up took more than thirty. By the time they reached the foot of the slope that led up to the shack the final strands of daylight were succumbing to the gloom of evening. The climb up was difficult; fifteen feet of deep snow covered with frost and thin ice which crackled with each step. One slip and there would be no escape. A man would gather momentum and slide over the edge in an instant. He held out his hand to Anne. After all they'd been through he didn't want to lose her now. She took it and, hand in hand, they gained the level ground.

There was a light in the shack, the glow of the paraffin lamp by which Anne had conducted the operation on a dead man. Jess wondered if Ezra was inside, if he'd returned suspecting they would come back for the horses. Perhaps, even now as they lay in the snow, he was sighting down the barrel of his rifle, waiting for them to raise their heads higher to give him a bigger target.

Anne made a suggestion. 'Why don't we wait in the shelter with the horses,' she said. 'He's already fed them.

146

He won't go back there tonight.'

Jess nodded his agreement. It would certainly be warmer in among the beasts. 'We'll go around the back of the shack,' he said. 'Follow the tracks we made when we made our escape. If he's inside he's less likely to hear us.'

Carefully, Jess again stepping in Anne's footprints, they made their way to the building in which the horses were stabled. The animals began making a commotion, jostling each other and snickering at the scent of approaching humans. The shack they were in didn't have a proper door; a length of thin leather covered the opening and was tied at the bottom and half way to pegs either side of the frame. Anne undid one of the bottom ties and crawled underneath. Jess paused for a moment, thinking he would investigate the other shack, find out if Ezra was there. He took a couple of steps in that direction.

Anne's voice called to him. 'Jess. Where are you?' And at the same time a rifle bullet struck the hut, sending the horses into a frenzy of excitement.

'Stay inside,' ordered Jess as he scuttled behind the stable.

Two more rifle rounds followed him, singing through the air on their way to smack solidly into the rock face beyond. Ezra's voice followed, his taunts and threats more evident in the tone than in the words. 'Got you cornered, boy. No escape this time. When I've killed you I'll find that girl and kill her, too.'

Instinct had governed Jess's choice to stay outside the stable and, as he pressed himself against the cold, wet wood of the building, the justification for that choice became clear in his mind. Despite Ezra's taunt, he wasn't cornered, but he would have been if he'd gone inside the stable. True, the lack of cover didn't give him much hope of escaping Ezra's gun but he might be able to draw him far enough away from the stable to give Anne a chance for freedom. He peered around the edge of the stable and immediately a chunk of wood flew up and over his head as a bullet struck a thick, corner stanchion. He raised his gun to return fire but knew he couldn't afford to waste shots. If he'd counted correctly, he'd fired four shots, which meant he should have two left. He broke the barrel and saw there was only one bullet left. His father, he remembered, always kept the chamber under the hammer empty to avoid an accidental discharge. Jess accepted the situation with equanimity – one shot or two, it didn't really matter because it was unlikely he'd get close enough to Ezra for his pistol to be effective.

The shadows of the rock face never looked so far away as they now did for Jess. He was trying to chart a path away from the stable that would keep Ezra hunting for him long enough for Anne to escape. The longer he considered it the greater was his certainty that no path existed. The moment he broke from cover, Ezra would shoot him. Then Anne would be at his mercy. He chanced another look to pinpoint Ezra's position. This time no shots came but Ezra was crossing the open expanse from the ridge to the stable with a determined stride, rifle at the ready. Jess figured that the lack of return gunfire had convinced Ezra that his opponent was either unarmed or out of ammunition.

'Anne,' he spoke huskily. 'Get on a horse. When you hear gunfire just ride. Keep your head down and ride as far and as fast as you can.' As he spoke he pressed against the stable wall as though hoping for one last time to be able to touch Anne Hames. As with the rear wall of the shack from which earlier they'd escaped, the timber of the stable was old and damp. Under pressure, Jess could feel it give and crumble. He pressed harder, forming a hole at shoulder height, a hole large enough to put his foot in.

'Come on, kid,' called Ezra Clayton, the sound of his voice suggesting he was no more than ten yards away on the other side of the stable. 'Come and face me. You killed my brothers and you're gonna pay for that.'

A cross beam, waist high, ran the length of the stable. Jess raised his right foot to it, got not much more than his toes on it, felt his boot sliding on the snow and ice that had settled there but pulled himself up regardless, knowing that this was his only hope of survival. Although his footing was insecure he continued scaling the back wall, his left foot finding the hole he'd recently created and he hauled himself silently onto the roof, rolling in the deep snow that lay there. No sooner had his legs come over the top than rifle fire sounded below.

Ezra cursed when he discovered that Jess wasn't behind the stable where he'd expected him to be. He stepped back, looked across to the mountain wall but saw no sign of his quarry. The horses in the stable were restless, anxious because of the gunfire. 'You in there, boy?' Ezra yelled and fired a shot in the air to announce his intention.

Jess knelt on the roof, his pistol pointed at Ezra's head, Dan Hathaway's words filling his mind: *If the time comes you have to kill him then don't hesitate. Just do it.* 'I'm here,' he said, then pulled the trigger. Simultaneously, Ezra fired, the sound of the rifle shot overpowering the report from the pistol.

In the tight little stable where cold, nervous animals vied with each other to be furthest from the tumult outside, Anne waited. She had heard Jess's instruction from beyond the wall, to mount a horse and ride as far and fast as possible, but she hadn't had time to act upon it. The gunshots had happened almost immediately after. Two, then one. Now, outside, all seemed silent. She feared for Jess's safety and if he was dead she knew it was only a matter of time before Ezra found her. She waited. Minutes passed and no one came. At length, when the horses had ceased their commotion, she could wait no longer. She lifted the bottom corner of the leather and looked around it. A body lay in the snow to her left. A rifle lay beside him. Jess Clarke stood over him, his arms at his sides, his pistol pointed at the ground.

'Jess!' He turned and she could see there was blood on his face, a line of it across his left cheek, of which he seemed unaware. 'You're hurt,' she said.

'They are all dead, Anne.' His voice registered surprise more than triumph.

She walked to him, took his arm and led him towards the stable. He walked unsteadily, his eyes seemed unfocused. For a while they sat in the stable without speaking. Eventually, Anne spoke. 'I thought you were dead.'

'He missed,' Jess replied. 'I didn't.'

'He didn't miss altogether,' she told him and used her handkerchief to absorb the blood that ran down his cheek.

He caught her hand and looked at the bloodstained handkerchief, then raised his hand to his cheek. 'I didn't know,' he said, staring at the blood that now showed on his fingertips as if that alone was proof of his injury.

'We should go up to the shack,' Anne said. 'My bag is up there with ointments and bandages.'

Jess didn't move, the events of the previous hours had sapped his strength. 'Let us sit here a while,' he said.

Anne sat close to him, from time to time tending to the gouge in his cheek with solemn intensity. Jess watched her face, noted with pleasure her care and concern. 'Is this what you intend to become? A doctor?'

She smiled, not the smile that warmed him in the way that nothing else in the world could warm him, nor the smile she had when she was teasing him and playful, but a smile of contentment, of certainty, of knowing what was good in her life. 'Yes.'

'You'll be a good doctor.'

'I'm going east come summer. Boston. Going to study at the same college as my father.'

'East,' he said, a trapdoor opening beneath his feet, the knowledge that, like Anne, his future was to emulate his father. Working the land was all he knew and he intended to excel at it as he knew she hoped to do as a doctor. His face betrayed his emotion.

'Doesn't mean I can't come back,' said Anne.

Jess stared at her for a moment, unsure if he understood her meaning, unsure if she was teasing him. There was a smile on her face that he hadn't seen before. 'Will you?'

'People in Wicker need a doctor. Place is getting too big for Pa to treat everyone.' She paused a moment, dabbed again at the blood on his cheek. 'Do you want me to come back?'

'Of course I do,' he said.

'Well then, that's settled.' They looked at each other for some time, he smiling, she waiting. 'I believe,' she said with a slight tone of impatience, 'that at times like this it is customary for a boy to kiss a girl.'

Jess moved towards her, put his arms around her shoulders and drew her to him. Then a rifle barrel pushed aside the leather flap and a man towered over them.

CHAPTER SIX

The three people looked at each other with equal amazement. Jess shouted, 'Dan!' And at the same moment Anne said, 'Mr Hathaway!'

Such was his surprise that more than one cuss word escaped Dan Hathaway before he recollected that one of the people present was a young girl. 'Sorry, Miss,' he apologized, 'but I wasn't sure I was gonna find you two alive.'

'You came looking for us?' said Jess.

' 'Course I did. You didn't think I was going to leave you in the hands of those Claytons, did you?' Then he explained how, when Charlie Bent had brought his message about the sick horse, he and Rory Blades had decided to wait for those in the rear to catch up rather than continue down to Two Falls Pass. Then they heard the multiple gunshots, which caused sufficient concern for Dan to turn back to investigate. 'Although we'd made pretty good time going down the mountain,' continued Dan, 'the weather changed at the same time as we heard those gunshots and snow began to fall again. It took the best part of an hour to reach Cal Brewster and the others and they told me about the killing of Reub Hadley and the arrival of the two horsemen. Cherokee Lil had recognized the Clayton twins, having often seen them in Butte. Their violent reputation was sufficient encouragement for her to say nothing when they were there, but when they'd gone she'd feared for your safety. I sent them on their way to join up with Rory and the others, then came in pursuit.'

'But how did you know where to find us?' asked Jess.

'Jess, boy, I know these mountains better than a purty woman knows her own face. When Cal Brewster told me which way they went I knew there was only two places they could be using. The other shack is higher up the mountain but closer to the trail from Missoula. I figured that would be the one they were using so I used an old Indian trail that I figured would get me there before you. Only I'd figured wrong. I'd picked the wrong cabin. Feared you'd be dead by the time I got here. Especially when I heard the gunfire.'

'They were gonna kill us,' said Jess, 'but I kept remembering your words that some men just need killing and when they do, don't hesitate. Just do it.'

Dan nodded. He turned his head in the direction of the body that lay outside in the snow. Although they couldn't see him, Dan said, 'That's Ezra Clayton. Where are the others?'

'They're all dead,' said Jess. 'Two of them are up at the shack. The other one went off the mountain.'

Dan looked at him hard, like he was trying to read Jess's mind, seeking the truth behind the answers he was about to give. 'You do it?'

Jess looked at Anne. 'We did it,' he said.

'Not the one outside,' explained Anne. 'Jess killed him on his own. Shot him with just a pistol against a rifle.'

'Nor the old one up at the shack,' said Jess. 'He was dying when we got here. He'd been shot clean through.'

'He was the one they wanted you to fix up.'

Dan's words didn't come out as a question but Anne Hames felt they needed an answer. 'There was nothing I could do for him. Nothing anybody could have done for him the way that bullet went through him. I guess he must have been a strong man to have travelled so far with such an injury.'

'What about Clay Brascoe?' Dan asked. 'Is he dead, too?'

'Clay Brascoe?' Jess and Anne looked searchingly at each other. 'He's not here.'

'We haven't seen him since we parted from the group.'

'Well he's around somewhere,' grumbled Dan. He spat on the ground. The very thought of Clay Brascoe brought a bad taste to his mouth. 'Cherokee Lil wasn't the only one who recognized the Clayton twins,' he explained. 'Clay Brascoe knew them from his time in Butte and he also knew something that Cherokee Lil didn't.'

'The bank robbery at Missoula,' declared Jess.

'That's right, Jess. When Cherokee Lil told me how he'd manipulated you two into the hands of the Claytons I knew what he was after.'

Anne Hames, prickled by the suggestion that she had been tricked into attending a patient, interrupted him. 'I chose to come up here, Mr Hathaway. There was a wounded man. It was possible I could have saved his life.'

'Miss,' said Dan, 'you only think you chose to come here. Clay Brascoe talked you into a corner you couldn't get out of. And he did it deliberately. Not just to cause trouble, like he did with Hadley and Bradall, but because he wanted the twins to lead him to their hideout. He wants the money from the bank robbery and he would have killed everyone when he found you. Couldn't have been a better set-up for him. Kills everyone so there are no witnesses and keeps the money for himself.' He thought a moment. 'Might even have taken the bodies of the Claytons back to Wicker for the reward. Of course, he would claim he'd never set eyes on you or the stolen money. No one would believe him but it would be impossible to prove otherwise.'

'Where do you think he is?' Jess asked.

'Must have lost the trail when the snow fell. In which case he could be anywhere on the mountain, but, if like me he was close enough to hear all that shooting, it'll have pinpointed the location of the shack.'

Anne Hames fixed her eyes on the old mountain man. 'What do you suggest we do, Mr Hathaway?'

'It's getting dark,' he said, 'and the sensible thing would be to stay in the shelter of these cabins for the night, but, if you're willing, I'd rather head on down to Two Falls Pass. The old Indian trails are only one horse wide but they're less prone to drifting snow and avalanche paths. The other advantage is that Clay Brascoe won't even know of their existence so there is no possibility of running into him. He's the kind of man who kills from ambush so I'd prefer to avoid the trail that brought you here.'

156

Anne and Jess were happy to agree to anything Dan Hathaway suggested. The thought of spending a second night in the cave at Two Falls Pass pleased both because it meant they would be home, in Wicker, early next day.

'Talking of rewards,' chimed up Dan. 'Perhaps you want to take those bodies back to Wicker as proof that the Claytons are dead.' Anne and Jess exchanged looks. Neither spoke, both looking to Dan for suggestions. 'Won't be easy leading horses along narrow trails,' he said. 'Sheriff Grayson, I suppose, might just take my word for it that I've seen the bodies and he can come up and collect them when the thaw comes. Unless the wolves or carrion have got to them first.' He rubbed his chin. 'Of course, if we can find the stolen money everyone will be happy to get that back. Dare say there'll be a reward for its return.'

'That must be what's in the saddle-bags,' said Anne.

'Yeah!' said Jess. 'Up at the shack.'

'Right,' said Dan. 'While you two are saddling up, I'll go and get it.' He lifted the leather sheet and went off into the gloom.

Anne and Jess worked quickly, anxious to be away. 'I suppose we should bring these other horses with us,' said Anne.

'They'd die if they stayed here,' agreed Jess, but he thought of Dan telling them it would be difficult to lead horses along the Indian trails. Still, he attached long ropes to their bridles and led them all out onto the open mountainside.

Anne Hames was securing two of the ropes to her saddle-horn and Jess was doing likewise when Dan emerged from the shack. His long, fringed buckskin coat flapped in the wind. His coonskin hat was pulled low on his head. In his right hand he held his rifle, across his left shoulder he'd slung the leather saddle-bags. He stepped forward, two steps, then a voice carried across the expanse of snow.

Clay Brascoe rose from where he'd lain in the snow awaiting his opportunity. 'I told you, old man, that only one of us would be coming off this mountain alive.' He pulled the trigger and Dan Hathaway stumbled backwards, knees buckling as though unable, any longer, to bear the load of his body. He went down, flat on his back and didn't move.

Jess Clarke yelled. 'Dan!' and ran towards his stricken friend.

'Stand still, lad,' shouted Clay Brascoe and he fired a bullet into the snow a yard ahead of him. 'You. Girl.' There was cruelty and triumph in his tone. 'Come here.' Anne didn't move. She remained by the horses, her senses numbed because it seemed that all they'd overcome was to no avail. Brascoe fired again, the shot kicking up snow even closer to Jess. 'Come here,' he ordered again, 'unless you want the next one to finish him.'

Slowly, the hair that had escaped from under her hat whipping around her face, she moved towards him. When she was close enough, he gripped her arm and pulled her towards him. 'Where are the twins?' He asked.

'Dead,' she told him. He didn't believe her. She pointed behind her, towards the stable, towards the shape in the snow. 'That's one of them,' she said defiantly. His expression was quizzical, unable to accept the truth of her words. 'The others are in that shack.'

A smile spread slowly across his face. 'Better and better,' he said. 'You,' he called to Jess, 'is the bank money in those saddle-bags?' Jess nodded. Clay Brascoe spoke again to Anne. 'You've done everything for me; found the money, killed the Claytons and led me to that old man. Such a pity that I can't reward you.' He laughed. He flipped the rifle in his hand so that the barrel now rested against Anne's temple. 'Get the saddle-bags,' he told Jess.

Jess was without option. He walked slowly, with deliberate stride to where his friend lay. Dan's eyes were open, watching his approach. When Jess bent to pick up the money, Dan whispered, 'The bullet hit the saddle-bags. Couldn't penetrate the coins. The force knocked me off my feet.'

Clay Brascoe shouted. 'Hurry. And don't try anything foolish. Leave that rifle on the ground.'

As he straightened, Jess whispered, 'I'll try to distract him.'

He turned, a scattering of coins fell to the ground. Jess bent, picked them up, held up his hand to show the money to Brascoe. 'There's a hole in it,' he explained, holding up the leather pouches, and he began walking, away from the shack, towards the stable.

Clay Brascoe thrust Anne Hames away from him and fired a bullet into the snow in front of Jess. 'Where do you think you're going?' he yelled.

'There are saddle-bags on my horse,' Jess told him. I was going to put the money in there. That way you won't lose any.' He began walking again.

Clay Brascoe stood silently, bemused. Was it a trick or was the boy as simple minded as the Claytons? Did he hope such consideration would earn mercy?

While Clay pondered, he watched Jess. He paid no attention at all to the movement away to his right. Dan Hathaway's fingers reached the trigger guard of his rifle and drew it slowly towards him. When it was firmly in his grasp he sat up. 'Brascoe,' he said, his voice low and distinct, ringing like a knell, a chilling sound of finality.

Clay Brascoe half turned. Dan Hathaway allowed him time to know his killer. Then he pulled the trigger and Clay Brascoe fell dead in the snow. Jess ran to Anne and held her close to him.

They watched Dan Hathaway as he stood over Clay Brascoe's body. 'Clay Brascoe,' he said, almost, Jess thought, as though announcing his arrival at a gathering where he was expected, and yet it was something more significant than that, as though he were telling whoever now laid claim to him that they were welcome to Clay Brascoe, that this world was finished with him. Then Dan put the toe of his boot under Brascoe and heaved him onto the steepest part of the slope. The body slid, gathered speed then sailed over the edge into the chasm beyond. Once more a recollection of Dan's words filled Jess's mind: *I'll forget your name the moment I kick your carcass off the mountain.*

With the body still in the air Dan Hathaway walked back to the young couple. He was smiling. 'Time to go home,' he said.